His Truth

His Guardians Book 7

By

Ronna M. Bacon

Verses to remember

2 Timothy 2:15. Do your best to present yourself to God as one approved, a worker who does not need to be ashamed and who correctly handles the word of truth.

Psalms 25:5. Guide me in your truth and teach me, for you are God my Savior, and my hope is in you all day long.

Table of Contents

He watched and listened as she taught her seminar, wondering how he would find the program he had learned she had written. It would be worth a lot of money if he could find it. He knew he would have buyers waiting for it, lined up, and he could sell it to the highest bidder.

The woman at the front of the room looked around, uncomfortable for some reason. Then, she shrugged and went on with what she was saying.

Later, she hurried to her vehicle, glancing around her. She could feel someone watching her, could feel the evil approaching her. Who was it, Lord, she thought? Who was the one who was after her? She had nothing that anyone would want.

He watched from the shadows as she almost ran to her car and drove away. He followed her, wanting to know where she lived. He would search her home and computer. He would have that program at some point, even if it meant she had to die for him to have it. He would devise a plan to get what he wanted, and it would start that very week.

Chapter 1

Watching the clouds float by in the autumn sky, Micah O'Connor hesitated before he opened the door to the conference building. He needed to be at this seminar, but he wished he didn't. Today would be the perfect day for being outside somewhere. He found a seat at the very back of the room and looked around, nodding to friends and acquaintances gathered. He leafed through the material provided. He wasn't sure that this would be productive in his position as computer specialist at Rebel's Elite Security, but his team leader, Abe Finlay, had asked him to attend. Just how do you find a suspect using a family tree, he wondered, then sighed. Lord, I need to change my attitude. You've put me here today, help me to learn.

He looked around as the seminar started, and then caught what the instructor was saying. Eyes narrowing, he just couldn't believe what he was hearing. Who was this teacher and how did he ever get to this position? He turned his head slightly as he heard soft movement beside him. A young woman stood there, dressed in jeans and a turtleneck sweater. A slight smile played on her face, and he wondered what she was thinking.

"Okay, Kat, I see you back there, just wanting to jump in. Come on up and help me get out of this jam."

Kat, the woman beside him, gave a soft laugh as she moved to the front of the room. "Why, Bob? You're doing so well. You don't need my help to dig the hole any deeper for yourself."

Bob Thomas, the instructor, shook his finger at her. "You know, we usually have one person question me. Today, no one did. That tells me they either tuned me out or are afraid to speak up."

"Probably both."

Laughter ran through the room at that. They realized they have been had and were eager now to learn.

"You see, folks, how easy it is to get led down the wrong path? You know Bob. You trust him. But someone should have spoken up and questioned his method. Now, let's start over." She tossed Bob a piece of chalk. "Get writing, because these people are going to work."

"This lady is really your instructor for today, folks. Kataleen Evans will be teaching family tree stuff for the next year at the college. She also serves as a family tree investigator and works as a consultant to police forces worldwide. You're in for a treat, people."

Micah had to admit, they had worked. Kat had been able to draw almost all of them into the discussion, including himself. He had found it interesting that she used a family tree to connect a suspect and a witness and then provide further information on the suspect.

"So, just to wrap up, folks. Family trees are out there to be used. If you can find information on people who are dead, then that can lead you to people who are alive. Family trees are wonderful. A lot of them are viewable to the public, just the living people are not named. Family trees will contain obituaries which are a wonderful source of information. That's it. If you have any questions for Bob or myself, our contact information is contained in your handouts."

Micah slowly gathered his material, lost in thought. So, how could he use this with the security team? He would have to think it through. It would be a good discussion to have with the team. They should have all been here today, he thought.

He slipped his sunglasses down on his nose as he headed for his truck. Not sure what to do with his time now, he paused, then nodded. A meal at Mac's, a local café, sounded good.

"Now, who would do that?"

Frustration in the voice beside him caught his attention, and he looked to see Kat, the instructor, standing about ten feet from him. He followed her line of sight and shook his head. A flat tire or two, he thought, from the way the car was leaning to one side.

"Can I help you?" His voice was quiet, but it still startled the young woman.

She spun, hand on her chest. "Sure, and be scaring the living daylights out of me, now would you?"

Micah grinned. "I'm sorry. I didn't mean to. But, can I help you?" He walked towards her car and then around it. "Looks as if it's just the two. I can call someone for you."

Kat studied the car, then Micah. "Thank you. I would hate to call Greg when I know he's planning on spending time with his kids today."

"Greg?"

She nodded. "My cousin, Greg Evans."

"Okay. I know Greg. No, let's not call him." Micah pulled out his phone, then looked up. "I can call a tow company that I know and have your car taken to a local garage. They'll have you fixed up in no time."

"Thank you. I would appreciate that."

Micah watched as she shivered, running her hands up and down her arms, then looking around.

"Are you okay?"

His quiet question once more caught her off guard. "I really don't know. I never did catch you name."

"It's Micah O'Connor and I work for Rebel's Elite Security."

She studied him. "Abe Finlay's team. Greg has spoken highly of all of Abe's men. I am pleased to meet you." She turned once more and looked around her.

Micah studied her, then looked around as well. He could feel eyes on them, but couldn't see anyone. "If you feel more comfortable, you can wait in my truck."

She turned, opened her mouth, then shook her head. "Thank you, if you don't mind. I just don't like the feeling I'm getting out here in the open. I've had it before and it never is a good feeling."

Micah hit his key fob to unlock the door for her. "It's that gray truck over there. I'll call for the tow and then be right there." He hesitated, then continued. "If you feel more comfortable, lock the doors after you get in." He turned to his phone, calling the tow company that Leah, one of the team's fiancées, worked for.

Kat headed for the truck, then felt a sudden tug on her briefcase. She gave a small cry as she tumbled to the ground, hitting hard on the asphalt.

Micah turned at her cry and watched as a dark-clad form raced from the area. He ran for Kat, dropping to kneel beside her. "Are you okay?" He scanned her for any injuries.

She sat up, dusting off her hands. "I am. Just angry. Why would he want my briefcase? It only held the notes from today's presentation. No laptop. No phone. Nothing but that paperwork."

Micah took in the ruffled red-gold hair and angry blue-green eyes and shook his head as he helped her to her feet. "I have no idea.

You're sure you're not hurt?" When she nodded, he pointed to his vehicle. "Come, let's get you tucked away. Then I'll call it in."

Micah paced as he waited for the patrol officer to appear. He studied Kat's car, then the direction her assailant had run. Were the two incidents related?

He turned at the sound of a diesel engine, then approached the tow truck as Smitty climbed down.

Smitty grinned, then frowned as he looked at Micah, then at the car. "More trouble has found one of you, has it?"

"It looks like it, Smitty. I thought at first it was just vandals, but the lady who owns that car just had her briefcase stolen."

"And you just happened to be here?"

Micah shook his head. "I was at a seminar she had just given and was heading out when I stopped to help. I guess you could say the Lord put me here." He turned as he heard a vehicle approaching. Good, he thought. Now, once our statements are done, I'll get her out of here.

Micah slid behind the wheel of his truck later and watched as Smitty pulled away. He turned to Kat, saw the fatigue in her face, and then hesitated.

"What were you going to say, Micah?" Kat turned to him. "I could see the hesitation."

"I'm going to take you over to the garage Smitty's heading for. It belongs to an uncle of another friend's fiancée. Once we've been there and found out what Gregor can do for you today, would you like to get some lunch? It's past that time now."

She stared through the windshield, not quite sure what to say. "I've taken enough of your time, Micah. I'm sure you have other things to do today."

"Nothing that is important enough that I abandon someone who needs help. That's not whom I am. That's not what I do." Micah's clear gray eyes stared back at her.

She finally nodded. "As long as it's something simple. This has taken my appetite."

Micah gave a soft laugh. "Yes, it would. And I would like to know what you meant about this not being the first time this has happened to you."

She gave him a startled glance. "Did I really say that?"

He nodded. "You did, and I would like
to help you if I can."

Chapter 2

Abe watched as Micah walked away from his truck, papers in hand, headed for the business office.

"Micah, how was the seminar?" Abe's call caught his attention.

Micah turned and waited for Abe to catch up with him. "It was interesting," he said. "I wasn't too sure at the beginning, but there's a lot of thinking to do about this. I have to figure out if any of it will work with us." Micah went on to explain what the seminar had entailed.

Abe watched Micah's face intently as he listened. There's something else going on here, Lord, and I have no clue as to what it is. I'm glad you do.

"Think it through and then we'll talk." Abe turned to walk away when he heard Micah say something more. "What was that, Micah?"

"I said that the instructor was Kataleen Evans, Greg's cousin. She had an incident in the parking lot. Two of her car tires were slashed, and her briefcase was stolen out of her hand."

Abe turned. "How is this related to the seminar?"

Micah shrugged. "I have no idea, and she doesn't either. She said there was nothing in the briefcase that was important. She does work as a consultant to police departments."

Abe nodded. "That could be a link. Are you planning on following up on that?" A spark of mischief peeked out of Abe's eyes as a grin spread across his face.

Micah shook his head at the teasing. "Not likely. The patrol officer seemed to have it under control."

Greg Evans watched as his cousin paced his living room, lost in thought. She had told him what had happened that afternoon. He just thanked God that she was all right and that Micah had been there. Only the good Lord knows what might have happened otherwise, he thought.

"Okay, Kat. Sit. Let's talk this over." Greg watched as she turned, her face clearing as she heard his words.

"I just don't understand it, Greg. Did they really think I had something in my briefcase?" She perched on the edge of the couch, a frown now marring her face.

"I don't know, Kat. I know you don't carry work around with you when you're at seminars. And you say you didn't have your laptop?"

She shook her head as the doorbell rang. "Your place is a busy place, isn't it?" she asked as she heard Mary greeting someone.

Greg stood and reached to shake the hand of Frankie Brennan, one of the town's police detectives. "What brings you out tonight, Frankie?"

"She does," he replied as he pointed at Kat. "I heard she had some excitement today."

"What excitement? Isn't that everyday life in a big city?" she retorted.

"Not for our friends, it isn't." Frankie sat in one of the armchairs, then pulled out his pad and pen. "Talk me through what happened. I have the reports both you and Micah gave.”

Kat stared at him. “Of course, Micah. You would know him.”

Frankie laughed at her comment. “That I do. I consider all Abe’s team good friends. Now, what happened? Talk to me. Tell me what you saw, what you felt, what you thought.”

Kat studied the wall behind him, eyes not really focusing as she went back through the morning up to the time the patrol officer arrived. “I felt someone watching me, Frankie. I couldn’t see anyone.”

“Was this before or after your briefcase was taken?”

“Before. I think Micah sensed something. He told me to go wait in his truck, unlocked it for me, and it was when I was walking over to it, that the man came at me and knocked me down.” She looked at the faint scrapings on her hands. “Micah was there right away.” She looked at him. “Who was it, Frankie?”

“We don’t know as yet. We’ve pulled surveillance video, gone over your car for fingerprints. By the way, Gregor says he’ll drop it off for you either late night or tomorrow morning."

"He doesn't have to do that." She was shocked. That kind of service she expected in her home town, but not here.

"He wants to, or rather Lydia does. It gives her an excuse to come out this way and then head on out to see Ian."

"Ian?"

Greg started laughing. "I see we'll have to make up a chart for you of who's who, Kat. Leah is engaged to Ian, one of Abe's team."

Kat threw her hands in the air. "I just can't get it all. Frankie, did you find my briefcase?"

He nodded. "It was found a few blocks from the centre, empty. We have it in evidence now."

"Of course, it was." She stood and paced once again. "This is so bizarre. Who would be after me here, in Riverville? I only moved here this week."

"Somehow, Kataleen, I don't think it's related to here. It's something in the past. We'll need you to go over the investigations you've helped with that resulted in a threat against you."

Greg turned his eyes to his cousin. "Threat? When did this happen?"

"In the past, Greg, and these people are in jail. When the cases were looked at in the past three months, it was determined there were no threats now."

"That may be, Kat, but I do know that sometimes people hide their feelings and still come after a person months and years later."

She sighed, then glanced towards the kitchen where she could hear Mary and the two children. "I know, Greg. That's why I think I need to move into my own place sooner than later. I don't want the threats involving your family."

Greg shared a long look with Frankie. Neither of them liked the idea of her living on her own, but then neither liked the idea of her living with Greg and, as she said, putting his family in danger. "When is your house ready, Kat?"

"Tuesday. Dad said the load of furniture would be here then as well." She worried her lower lip with her teeth, then sighed. "I didn't plan this very well, I don't think. I have to find someone to help me move the furniture and boxes in, and you're away next week."

Greg started to laugh, and she turned to glare at him. "Don't worry, KitKat. God has already provided help for you. When I talked to Abe last week about you moving here, he mentioned his team would be willing to help lift and carry."

She stared at him, lost in thought for a moment. Then her face cleared. "Yes, that will work. Are we done now, Frankie?"

Frankie nodded, a little confused at the abrupt changes in the conversation. "If I have further questions, I'll track you down." He watched as she walked rapidly from the room.

Greg was laughing as he turned his eyes back to him. "She's one of a kind, Frankie. Takes a bit of getting used to, she does."

"That she does. Tell me, does she have a boyfriend back home, someone she just broke up with, any threats or letters along that line I should know about?"

Greg shook his head. "She's never really dated. Guys are put off by her intelligence and outspokenness. She's always been like that. If someone had threatened her or her family, she would have dealt with it right then and there, not let it lie silent and fester."

"That's good to know. I'll have a team go through her office at the college, just as a precaution." Frankie snuck a peek back at the door to the kitchen, then grinned at Greg. "Any chance Micah will be helping on Tuesday?"

Greg laughed even harder at this. "I can ask. You're thinking along the same lines as I am."

Frankie just grinned as he headed for the door. "Keep me updated if she says anything about someone threatening her. Right now, we don't have a lot to go on."

Nathaniel watched as Micah stared at his computer monitor, not moving. He tilted his head to study his friend's face, then leaned his head back as he felt a paper wad hit his arm. Ian was watching Micah as well, and when Nathaniel looked over at him, grinned. They both had the same thought, that whoever had caught Micah's interest must be special. Abe, looking up from his own paperwork, studied the three men, then shook his head. Lord, I know they want Micah to be as happy as they are. If it's

Greg's cousin, then You'll have to work it out.

"Okay, fellows. Greg called. His cousin needs some help moving into her own place on Tuesday. We can't all make it due to training, but Micah, you, Matt and Ian are nominated to go help."

Micah turned in his chair to stare at Abe. "Just like that? We're nominated? No asking if we want to?"

Abe held up his hands. "I'm sorry, Micah. I didn't phrase that right, did I? Greg asked if any of us could help. You three are the ones not doing any training with the new group in next week. Would you three consider helping out?"

Micah kept watching Abe, not saying anything. Ian and Nathaniel watched with interest the staring match between the two men, and then grinned at each other with Micah finally nodded. It would be an interesting day, they thought.

Chapter 3

Carrying in one of the last boxes from the truck, Micah looked around for Kat.

"Where do you want this one?"

She stared at him, lost in thought, then shook her head. "In the room I've designated as the office, please. Tell me that's the end of it?"

Micah nodded. "Just about. There's only three or four more boxes."

"Good. Can I order in something for you fellows to eat? Mary's heading home with the two kids to get them settled for supper and then bed."

Ian and Matt shook their heads as they walked by, heading for her office. "We're good, thanks. Our ladies are expecting us shortly for a meal."

Kat turned to look at Micah, who nodded. "Or we could head over to Mac's for a meal."

Kat nodded. "I would rather just order something. Where's a good place to order from?"

"Mac's." Micah laughed at the expression on her face. "I just have to say it's for us and he'll deliver it himself."

She shrugged, then walked to the door to thank the other two men as they left. Suppressing a sigh, she turned to survey her living room and the rest of her new home. Boxes were stacked everywhere, but at least the furniture had been placed where she wanted it.

Micah stood leaning against a door frame, watching the emotions flickering across her face. She needed to sit, and he didn't know it he could get her to do that.

She turned, feeling his eyes on her. "Okay, Micah. You've ordered our meal, I gather. If you want to start unpacking books in the office, I'll start in the kitchen."

He pushed away from where he had been standing, walked over, and hands on her shoulders, shoved her down on the couch. She glared up at him, then relaxed.

"Thank you. I don't know if I could have stood up any more."

He nodded as he sat on the floor in front of her and pulled off her sneakers and socks. "You need to put your feet up for a while. As to the boxes, leave them for tomorrow if you can. Some of the guys' ladies are heading this way to help you unpack." He absentmindedly rubbed her ankles as he talked.

"Why?"

"Why what?"

"Why come help me unpack? I don't know them."

"Not yet, you don't but you will. They're all good friends with Mary and you'll be part of their group, if you want. They really do want to get to know you." He paused, tilting his head to watch her. "That's if you do. We would really like it if you would. We also get together as ladies and guys for separate Bible study. They want you as part of that as well."

Kat leaned her head back on the couch and closed her eyes. "I haven't been part of a ladies' study group since college. They usually meet during the day when I can't."

"These ladies all work as well. They meet on a Thursday evening, I think."

"Why, Micah? Why do they want this?"

He shrugged, not quite sure how to answer. He rose as the doorbell rang. Kat headed for the kitchen, trying to remember what box she had the cutlery and plates in.

Micah stopped her with a hand to her arm. "Mac sent all we need, food, plates, and cutlery."

She turned. "Why, Micah? He doesn't know me."

"No, but he knows me, and now he considers you my friend."

She shook her head. "I don't know about this town, Micah. What's with everyone being so friendly?"

"Isn't it like this where you come from?" He was genuinely puzzled.

She nodded. "But we're a small town and it's expected."

She paused as Micah gave thanks for their food, then looked at him again, sighing as her phone chimed with a text message. It had been chiming off and on all day, and she had managed to ignore it.

"Aren't you going to check your messages?" Micah pointed his fork at her phone.

"I usually don't if someone's around. I find the person I'm with is more important than messages. But if it's okay with you, it's probably just my folks checking in."

She pulled up her text messages and starting to scroll through them, smiling at her folks' messages. Then, she stopped at the next message and froze. How did he find her phone number?

Micah moved over beside her and gently took the phone from her hand, reading the message.

"Do you get a lot like this one?"

She shook her head. "Every once in a while, I get something from someone. They usually are nothing. I pass them on to the police and they work through them." She looked over at him, disturbed at the grim look on his face. "Micah, it happens. I accept it as part of the risks of what I do."

"But you work in the background, don't you? How do they know who you are?"

She shrugged. "Cops talk. People overhear. I've had to testify in court. That's how things get out." She took back her phone and stared at the screen. "Though, I haven't had one of these in a long time. God has protected me from that, I would say."

She turned to him. "You need to get on your way, Micah. Thank you for helping today."

He stood, staring down at her. "No, thank you, Kat. I enjoyed myself. Come, lock up after me. By the way, I'm going to ask Joseph to stop by and take a look at how to improve your security, if I can. He's our security expert."

She studied him, seeing the care and concern and yes worry in his eyes. She then nodded. "If it makes you feel better, then you can."

She locked the door, then leaned back against it as she listened to his footsteps fading down the walk. Why, Lord, did you bring such an interesting gentleman into my life in a town I'm only staying in for a year? Are You trying to tell me something?

The watcher stood across the street from her home, hidden by the shrubs and fencing. He noted Micah leaving, then turned his eyes back to her home. He had been able to get in and go through it before she moved in. Soon, he thought. Soon, he would find what she had hidden from him. He would find a way.

Frankie looked up as Micah knocked at his door, then glanced at the clock. Micah wasn't usually in town at this time of day if there was a team in training at their facility.

"Micah, what can I do for you?"

Micah shook his head as he sat. "She's not going to like me doing this, I can already tell that."

"Who's not going to like you doing what?" Frankie was amused at the riddle Micah was spinning.

"Kat. Some of us helped move her things into her house today. I stayed for a meal with her afterwards. She got a nasty text message, Frankie, and that concerns me enough to come talk to you."

"Did you read it?"

Micah nodded. "I did. It was a threat. Somehow, this person found her phone number, and is threatening her life if she doesn't hand over something. She just shrugged it off."

Frankie watched the concern flickering across Micah's face. You were right again,

Deirdre, he commended his wife silently. Micah does have it bad.

"Did she say what she would do about it?"

Micah shrugged. "I don't think she'll do anything, and I don't like that, not after what happened the other day."

Frankie leaned back in his chair and sighed. "And now I must follow up with her, given that you've been here. How do I do that without giving away you were?"

Micah shrugged, then grinned. "That's your problem, Frankie. This may well be part and parcel of what happened to her the other day. I would hate to see anyone hurt if we can help it."

Frankie studied Micah once again. "Are you saying that because of your concern for her or because you've seen this in the past?"

"Nothing in the past, Frankie. I haven't had the problems or adventures or what you would like to call it that the others did. Very stable home life, two parents, two brothers, many pets."

Frankie shook his head at him. "For once, we don't have to worry about something in your past coming up to haunt us then."

Micah gave him a puzzled look, then stood. "If you can find some way to talk to her, I would appreciate that."

Frankie looked down at his phone as it chimed. "I don't think I'll have to find a way. Your lady's calling me now."

"Catch you later then." Micah walked away, thinking back over their conversation. As his hand settled on the truck door handle, he stopped. What had Frankie meant, his lady?

Chapter 4

Kat watched as Frankie read the text message, then asked her permission to scroll through the rest she hadn't bothered to read. He paused again, then looked up at her.

"You haven't read past that one?" When she shook her head, he continued, "That wasn't the first one he sent. I'd like to forward them to myself. Then I can send them on to the crime lab and get them working on finding out who this person is."

"Go ahead. I don't think you'll find out who it is, and at this point, I don't think we'll have much to worry about."

Frankie shook his head. "I think you're wrong. Given what happened the other day and now these, I think we need to search through this. You're a stranger in town, and things like the other day, don't happen to strangers."

She turned to walk to the window, staring out into the gathering dusk. "I don't know who it would be. I haven't done any consulting work in at least a year. Unless it's related to the family tree consulting I've done, and I can't see that. There was nothing in any of them that I found that would warrant this." She turned to face him. "Send yourself those messages and see what you can find."

Frankie nodded, then handed her back her phone. "I'll let you know what I find out. If you get any more, call me."

As she set her phone down, it chimed again. She swiped to open it to the text message and then froze, her eyes flying to Frankie.

Concern coloured his face as he reached for her phone, read the message, then handing her back her phone, spun for the door and was out it without saying a word. She watched the closed door, waiting for what she didn't really know.

Frankie tapped, then opened the door to come in, speaking over his shoulder. It had been thirty minutes since she had received the text. Officers searching the neighbourhood had found no one but they had found the spot the man had stood in earlier.

"The neighbours are just going to love me. I just move in and have police activity already." She was concerned and ready to put all her goods back on a truck and move.

Frankie gave a laugh at her comment, then shook his head. "I know these people, Kataleen. They're good folks. They'll watch out for you and your home. Now, we didn't find the man, but we found where he had been standing. Our crime scene team going over that area right now." He blew out a breath. "I hate to ask when you've got boxes all over, but we need to search your home, just in case he's been in here."

She swallowed hard, uneasy at the thought, then nodded. "Sure, go ahead. I guess Micah was right when he said he'd have to have someone go over my security."

"Joseph?" At her nod, he continued, "Joseph will set you up all right for what you need, without making it feel like a fortress."

Micah laid his Bible back on the end table by his couch and sat back, contemplating what he had read on God's truth. Lord, we need to trust in You and Your truth. There is so much falseness and so many lies out there today. He thought back over the past few days, with the new group in for security training, the seminar. Then his mind wandered to Kataleen and he thought how she had brought in so much information into her teaching, almost more than an average person could handle.

He reached for his wallet lying on the table beside his Bible and pulled out her business card. He fingered it, trying to make up his mind whether to call her or not. He was concerned about her safety. He knew Frankie would be thorough, but they didn't have anything really to go on right now. He just had that feeling something was about to happen, and it was going to draw him into it, whether he wanted to or not.

He picked up his phone as it chimed. Funny that it would be Frankie calling him when he was thinking about him.

"Frankie, you're working late."

"Yeah, I am. Your lady got another text when I was there. Whoever it is was standing near her place watching her. He mentioned you, not by name, but as her gentleman caller."

"What?" Micah sat forward, hand going to his sandy-blond hair. "Where?"

"There's a nice little place hidden by fencing and shrubs where he could stand and watch the front of her house. The team figures he was there while you were helping her move in." Frankie's voice faded away for a minute, then came back stronger. "Listen, Micah. I've just gotten called in on another investigation, but I wanted to make sure you would be keeping in touch with her. Get Joseph over there as soon as you can. Her home security isn't very good."

"What home security? It's an older home, locks are cheap, no security system." Micah blew out a breath, then sighed. "But will she let us?"

"She will. I also talked to the home owner, who happens to be Mac. Did you know that?"

"Mac? No, I didn't. Then that means we can go ahead with whatever we need to do to make it safe."

"That you can. He's having new steel doors installed tomorrow as well as work done on the windows. He told me that Joseph is to install whatever he needs to and to send him the bill. He said he had just bought the house and had offered it to Greg, meaning to go over it this week himself."

"We'll do that. Frankie, that new text message? Did it threaten her?" Micah's voice was hesitant, not his usual strong voice.

Frankie stared at his phone for a moment. What happened to Micah? This was not him.

"No, it didn't directly. Kataleen says she hasn't worked for the police for about a year. We'll be in touch with those departments. The thing of it is, though, Micah, is that she consults on family tree searches and those she is adamant she will not breach their privacy to tell us who."

"So, it could be one of them, and we wouldn't know. Okay, thanks, Frankie."

Kat pulled the blanket up on her. She had curled up on her couch, too afraid to head for her bed. Who was it, she thought, jumping at every creak and groan of the house? Greg had called to check on her, but she hadn't told him about the text messages. It was bad enough he had had to find out about her car and her lost briefcase.

She laid her head back on the couch, her thoughts wandering through the day. A smile crossed her face, thinking of the men who had been there. They get along so well, she thought, a real team. Her thoughts then drifted to Micah. Then she shook her head. No, she didn't need anyone in her life. No one, just herself.

A knock at the door roused her the next morning, and she sat up, startled, unsure for a moment where she was. She stood, trying to untangle herself from her blanket, smoothing her hair back into her normal low ponytail as she headed for the door. Peeking out, she stared at the three younger women standing there.

As she opened the door, she saw a work truck pulling up as well. What was going on?

"Hi, you must be Kataleen. I'm Adriel. These two ladies are Leah and Elizabeth. We've come to help you today." Adriel watched Kat for a minute. "You do need help, don't you?"

Kat shook her head, then smiled. "I do. Come in. Sorry, I just woke up."

"And we're the ones who woke you." Leah's soft voice reached her ear. "Show me your kitchen and your coffee pot and I'll put on a pot while you go get yourself ready for the morning." She turned as the man approached from the work truck.

"Kataleen, this is Joshua Logan, renovator in town. Mac, who by the way owns your home, asked him to come do some work today to make it more secure. He hadn't had a chance to get the changes made, you were here too quick." Leah greeted

Joshua, then turned back to Kat. "Joshua is also brother to our police chief, Caleb, so you're in good hands."

By early afternoon, the ladies had left as had Joshua. Kat looked around her home, then headed for her office. She needed to get that set up the way she liked. College courses would be starting soon, and she needed to be ready. Then, she stopped, staring at the vase of roses on her desk, a frown in place. Where did these come from?

She walked over, searching for a card. Finding one, she fingered it for a minute as she touched the roses.

Opening it, she read: *"Glad you are here in my town. I would like to take you to dinner tonight, if I may. Micah"*

How sweet, she thought, looking around for her phone. Now, how do I get in touch with him. A thought hit her mind, and then smiling she scrolled through her contacts. Sure enough, he had entered his contact information last night. A swift text to him, and she turned to her office.

Joseph watched as Micah headed off that night, then turned to Matt. "Micah usually doesn't head to town after a training session. He's so intense with them, they wipe him out."

Matt laughed. "But he usually doesn't have a lady he wants to call on."

Joseph turned to Matt. "A lady? Really?"

"That's right, you weren't around last night. Micah apparently has an interest in Greg's cousin, Kataleen. I would hazard a guess that's where he's off to."

"Our Micah? Do we know this lady?" Joseph was on the defensive at once.

"Relax, Joseph. She's Greg's cousin. He can vouch for her."

Joseph shook his head. "I know. It's just hard to see Micah with a lady of his own. He's so quiet."

"He is, but then we all are, and look at the ladies God brought to us."

Joseph stared into the distance. "I just pray Micah doesn't go through what we did, Matt."

"Me, too. It was hard enough going through it, without watching all of the rest going through it." Matt turned to look back at the office. "Speaking of that, what's up with Abe? He's been looking distracted lately."

Joseph agreed. "I asked Murphy. He doesn't know either. I wish I knew how to help him. Prayer is what we'll have to do, Matt."

Kat brushed her coral sweater down over her jeans and pulled her hair tighter in the matching bow. I wish I had asked him where we were eating, she thought, as she slipped her bare feet into loafers. I may be way underdressed.

Hearing a knock at her door, she took a deep breath. It's just a friend, girl. Get yourself together. But somehow, she knew he was different from anyone she had met. God, is this You? Have You heard my prayers?

As Micah waited for Kat to open her new door, he scanned the area, zeroing in on where Frankie had found the evidence of the onlooker. He noted that Joshua had worked his magic with the doors and windows. Joseph was due to the next day to go over security with Kat, if she was around.

Kat stood watching Micah for a minute before he turned to face her. How do I always end up with such tall guys in my life, she thought? She smiled as he turned, closed and locked the door behind her, then hesitated as he held out his hand, giving him a searching look. At his shrug and grin, she shook her head and took his hand.

Later that evening, she locked the door and once more leaned against it, lost in thoughts, a dreamy look on her face. She had enjoyed her dinner with Micah and then the walk along the riverbank afterwards. He was so thoughtful. Checking to make sure the door was locked, she pushed away from it and headed for her office. She needed to get to work, but thoughts from the evening kept intruding.

Chapter 5

Assessing Kat's house the next day, Joseph listened to the conversation and teasing going on between Micah and Kat. He had to agree with Matt. Maybe this was the lady for Micah. He didn't know if he had heard Micah this carefree before, or if so, then it had been a long while. A little bit of subtle flirting going on there, he thought.

Joseph finally went to find Kat.

"Kat, I've done the assessment. Here's what we would like to do."

"We? Who's this we?" Kat turned to face him from where she had been shelving the books Micah was handing her.

"Mac and me. He wants everything up to date and as safe for you as it can be." At her look of protest, Joseph held up his hand. "Just listen, okay? Mac does this for any rental that he has. He installs security systems, new doors, windows, whatever it will take to keep his tenants safe."

Kat studied him for a minute, then shrugged. "I guess it's okay then. What do you need from me?"

"I'll need you to come up with a good password for the system. I'm heading out to get what I need. I should only be about thirty minutes or so. Want me to bring back lunch?"

Kat stared at the two men. "What is it with you two? Do you think I won't eat or something?"

Joseph shook his head as they laughed. "No, we don't think that. But we want to eat, and we won't eat in front of you without you having something."

"Then just a salad please. I normally don't eat a big lunch."

Micah turned to watch as Kat shelved the last of the books, then moved to break down the boxes. "Where do you want the boxes, Kat?"

"On the porch for now, Micah, thanks. I have to bundle them for pickup yet."

"Where's your tape or cord? I can do that for you."

Kat turned to stare at him once again, meeting his eyes, a puzzled look on her face.

Then she shook her head and moved away to find the cord and scissors for him. These two men were doing more for her than her father or brother ever did. She liked it in a way, but she didn't want to become dependent on them.

Micah turned from where he had been reading a framed poem. "I like that thought, Kat."

"What's that?"

"The fact that God is in control, He has a plan for us, we need to trust Him, and that His truth always come through."

She smiled as she realized which poem he had been reading. "Mary's sister, Miriam, wrote that a while ago, when I was going through a rough patch. I'm going to miss our lunches and conversations."

"You'll be back there before you know it." Micah realized he really didn't like the sounds of that. Now why, he wondered? "Have you had any more text messages?"

She shook her head. "That's how it always goes. I get three or four, then they stop."

Micah paused in his movement, his mind picking up on what she had said.

"You've had this before? From the same number?"

Kat's eyes widened, then she pulled out her phone. "I have the numbers stored that I get the calls from. Let me check."

As she scrolled through her phone, Micah's mind turned over what she had said. If she got them in series, and it was the same number, then someone was really trying to scare her.

Kat raised her head, a look of fright and worry on her face. "They are, Micah. I never thought of that, at least not to put it into words. Whenever it happened, the police always just shrugged it off."

Micah reached for her phone. "Is there a way to send this to Frankie? I can tell you right now that this is not going to be shoved aside. Frankie wouldn't do that to you. Nor would I. I don't like seeing that fright on your face."

She shivered suddenly. "I thought it was all in the past. Guess it isn't, is it? So now what happens, Micah?"

"I've sent the file to myself as well. I'm also going to send it on to an investigative company here in town, Tracker's. We used them as has the police.

They really good at finding people who don't want to be found."

She nodded as she wrapped her arms around herself. "This scares me, Micah. Who would be after me?" She dropped down into an upholstered armchair she had in her office, worry evident on her face.

Micah tucked his phone into his pocket, then came and crouched down in front of her, reaching for her hands. Startled she looked down at their hands, then at him.

"I won't let anyone hurt you, if I can at all help it, Kat." He bit his lip before continuing. "I think we need to talk to Abe and Frankie as well. From what I saw of the calls, they're coming more frequently, aren't they?" When she finally nodded, he dropped his head. "That's what I thought. Have you talked to anyone about these?"

She shook her head. "I reported the first few but the officer I talked to just blew it off. Since then, I just archived them and kept them there."

Micah nodded, then turned his head as Joseph came into the room. "Frankie will be here shortly to talk to you again. Given that someone was outside the other day watching you, we need to get an investigation on the way. Now, Joseph's back. Let's put this aside from now and see what he decided to bring us."

She sat for a minute, then let Micah pull her to her feet. Lord, why now? Why when I'm just setting up in a new town? Was I not to ever leave my home town? Is that the whole purpose of this?

Chapter 6

Frankie pocketed his note pad and pen as he watched Kat rubbing her hands up and down her arms. He was angry and trying not to show it. If the officer it had first been reported to had followed through with the investigation, then maybe he wouldn't have a woman sitting here in front of him scared, and a friend worried about his lady. He snuck a peek at Micah and nodded to himself. There was something going on there, he knew, just didn't know whether the two involved were aware yet.

"You'll be talking with Abe, Micah?"

Micah looked over at Frankie. "I will. This should have been stopped months ago."

Kat looked between the two men, then rose and walked away. She needed space before she said something she shouldn't. Joseph looked up from where he was finishing running wires and sensors at the back door.

"They're getting to you, are they?" He grinned at the disgruntled look on her face.

Then, she sighed. "They are, and I shouldn't let them. But I have never lived in fear, never felt a need to have all this stuff." She waved a hand around at the security system he was installing. "At home, we never locked our doors during the day. We never had to. If something was taken, then we knew who it was, and they paid for it or returned it."

"This is a big city, Kat, and a different lifestyle. Even where we live, outside of town, we lock up everything."

"That's different. Your area is a business. That's expected."

"Yes, it is. But you can't live in a city without taking precautions. Now, I've finished setting everything in place. Let me walk you through what I've done, and have you set your security code. Do you have someone you can give a key to, besides Mac, and have them set their own security code?"

"Greg, likely. Or is that a good idea?"

"Greg should be fine. What I would suggest though, is that you have one of us as a backup, just in case Greg is away and you need someone."

"So many decisions to make, Joseph. I don't know which one of you to have, though."

"Try Micah." He laughed at the look on her face. "Trust me. Micah would be happy to do this."

"Micah would be happy to do what?"

Kat's eyes slid closed as she realized Micah was right behind her.

Joseph was laughing as he responded. "I suggested Kat let you have a key to her place and set your own security code, just in case Greg is away and someone needs to get in here."

Micah watched Kat's profile, not sure if that would be a good idea. She turned to him, then nodded.

"It's okay. I'm just not happy with this whole scenario."

"We know you're not. Now, Frankie wants to speak with you."

"I'm sure he does. Thanks, Joseph. I appreciate all you've done." She walked away to find Frankie.

Micah eyed Joseph, who kept his face turned away from him, so he couldn't see the grin on his face.

"Now I know what you other guys felt like, you know that? Thanks a lot, Joseph." Micah was shaking his head as Joseph turned.

"You're welcome, Micah." Joseph stood, and then looked around Micah to find Kat. "Just so you know, she's interested." With that, he gathered up his tools and walked away.

Micah spun to watch him, remembering to close his mouth. Then, he too went to find Frankie, to find out what they would be doing to find the person responsible.

Kat turned from closing the door after Frankie and wandered through her house. She was alone again, and greatly afraid. Frankie's talk with her had not gone the way she planned. He was upfront with her, stating she was in danger. She frowned, not liking that word, then sighed. She couldn't let her father or brother know. They'd be there to pack her up and move her back to her home town. Part of taking this position had been to gain some freedom. She loved her family, but she needed to walk away for a time, to not feel smothered.

The next afternoon, she picked up the mail that had been brought in and dropped on her desk the day before. Flipping through it, she frowned as she looked at an envelope, then turned to look at the door. No, there was no way whoever was sending the text messages had now switched to letters.

Finding her letter opener, she slit the envelope and pulled out a card. A "to my sweetheart" card. She opened it and let out a small scream, then gathering it up and finding her purse, she ran for her car. She had to find Frankie. And then Micah. Dear Lord, she thought, protect him. Just because he helped me, he's now in danger? This can't be real. This can't be what I'm living.

Frankie looked up from his desk at a tap on his door. Eddie Brown stood there, looking towards the front of the building.

"Didn't you just speak with Greg's cousin, Kataleen?"

Frankie nodded, then slowly rose to go to the door. "I did. And now she's here?" He went forward to bring her back to his office and seated her, watching her intently. She was frightened, he could tell, but more frightened than she had been.

Her hands trembling, she handed over the envelop and card. "This was in my mail, Frankie. What is going on?"

Frankie motioned for Eddie to come in as he opened the card. Shock stopped him for a minute.

"When did you two go out for a meal?"

"The other night. He was following us and took that picture." Her eyes never left his face. "Frankie, Micah is in danger. How do I get him to stay away from me?"

"You won't, Kataleen." Eddie spoke up, bringing her eyes to his face. "Once he knows about this, and he will have to, he will not stay away. It's not in any of Abe's men to walk away when someone is in danger, even if it means putting their own lives at risk. It's who they are and what they do."

Kat slumped back on the hard back of the chair. "That's about what I thought you would say." She shook her head, frustration evident. "So, who is it?"

Eddie shared a glance with Frankie, then spoke. "When do you start teaching your class? And how often a week?"

"It starts a week from Monday and runs Mondays and Wednesdays. The rest of my days are filled with consulting like I always have done." She searched their faces. "Why?"

"We need to plan to ensure you are safe. I'll have an officer go over your classroom. Will you have an office on campus?"

She nodded. "I have to have for student access. You'll want him to go through that as well?"

Frankie nodded. "We will. I'll look after speaking with the college head and getting that sorted out. Joseph has finished with his upgrades?"

"He has." She rubbed her hands on her face, frustration evident to the two men. "I don't need this, you know. I suppose you'll be wanting to go back over every threat I've ever received?"

"We will. We'll need you to work through the names from your consulting business and pass them on to us. We'll have to have a court order for that, but that shouldn't be a problem." Frankie perched on the edge of his desk, fingers tapping on the top, as he thought, his gaze fixed on the opposite wall. "Tell me again, Kat. There is no old boyfriend, boyfriend wannabe, etc., in your life?"

"No boyfriend. I just haven't had the time to be involved with anyone. This career path of mine took a lot of time and dedication to get me to where I am now."

She stood, uncertainty in her movements. "I can leave now?"

Frankie nodded. "I'll be in touch."

Eddie watched her walk away, then turned back to Frankie, sitting down in the chair Kat had vacated. "What are your thoughts, Frankie?"

Frankie stared at Eddie for a minute, then shook his head. "If there had been an old boyfriend, I would say it was him. But there isn't. So, now what? We have threats, we have this picture with Micah crossed off, we have her denial of an old flame."

Eddie nodded, then rose. "You're on your way out to see Micah?"

Frankie nodded. "I have to."

Abe was on a hunt. Frankie was here to see Micah and he couldn't find him. His truck was in its spot.

Poking his head into the exercise building, he looked around, then yelled, "Anyone seen Micah?"

The team in for training that week spun to stare at him. Murphy and Ian took one look and were at his side, out the door with him.

"He's been around. What's wrong?" Ian was concerned enough to start scanning the area.

"Frankie's here. Kat got a card this morning that had a picture of Micah and her inside. Only Micah was crossed off." Abe's voice was grim.

"I don't like that, Abe. His truck's here, but he's not?"

Abe shook his head. "No one's seen him in the last little while, not since he finished his part of today's training. I checked his cabin. Not there."

Chapter 7

Micah stared at the masked man sitting on the rock across from him, rifle pointed at his heart. A standoff, he thought, and the only one who will get hurt is me. How did he get the drop on me? He knew. He had been out here walking, trying to clear his head, when he had walked right into this ambush. Lord, I have no idea where this is going, but I sure hope You have a plan.

"What do you want?" Micah demanded.

The man watching him shook his head, then glanced down at his watch. He kept doing that, Micah noted. If there is some way I can get to him, and disarm him, when he does that.

Micah waited, eyes glued to the man. He heard quiet footsteps behind him, then nothing as a blow to the head took him down. He didn't feel himself dragged off behind rocks and bound, didn't see the men leaving.

Abe searched the faces of the men in front of him. Micah wasn't there, and no one could find him. Abe's eyes turned to the rocks and hills around him. He knew Micah liked to get up there to think. Is that where he is, Lord, he asked. Lead us to him, please.

Frankie pocketed his phone as he moved towards Abe. "I have search and rescue teams on their way out, be about thirty minutes. Where do you want to start?"

Abe turned back to study his friend. "We'll pair up, Frankie, one of the trainees with one of my men. We need someone to run Micah's set up to keep us in contact." He turned to his team, eying each one. "Joseph, take Micah's spot. You're the one most familiar with the equipment." He took the com link he was handed and settled it in his ear. "Okay, one trainee with one of my team. Frankie, you're with me. Spread out in the rocks around us."

Micah groaned as he came to, trying to move his arms and legs. Then he lay still, looking around through blurry eyes. Night was coming, and he knew the temperature would be dropping. He peered at the sky. Just great, he thought, all I need. Rain.

Abe turned as Frankie touched his arm and pointed behind them. The search dogs had arrived. Rebecca, Abe's sister, had waited for them, handing them some of Micah's clothing. Lord, he prayed, let them find him fast.

Abe watched as the dogs worked through the path and then headed off in another direction, trying to find the scent.

"Which way would he have gone, Abe?" Frankie's question caught his attention.

"I really don't know, Frankie. He walks all the paths back here, and there are quite a few." Abe spun in a circle, trying to think of where Micah might have gone. "I just don't know."

Kat stopped her vehicle and watched the activity going on at Rebel's. She had come that way, needing to talk to Micah, and found this. She shut her car door and then walked towards the officers milling around.

Eddie saw her coming and walked towards her.

"What's going on?" Kat's presence surprised him.

"Frankie came looking for Micah, and they can't find him." Eddie watched as Kat's face paled, and he reached a hand out to steady her. He looked around, spying

Rebecca. "Come with me. I'll take you over to Abe's sister, Rebecca. You can wait with her."

Kat shook her head. "No, I shouldn't be here." She turned and walked back to her car, not seeing Rebecca come towards her.

Rebecca Andrews watched as Kat drove away, then turned to approach her uncle. "Eddie, who was that?"

"That was Kataleen Evans. She was out here looking for Micah."

Rebecca turned once more to watch the settling dust. "Oh, that Kat!"

Eddie gave a small laugh. "Yes, that Kat. Now what do we do with all these people?"

"Peg's on her way out and so are the guys' ladies. We're getting some sandwiches, coffee, what have you ready." She shivered and rubbed her arms. "I just hope it's not a long night."

Eddie swung an arm around his niece and directed her back to Abe's home. "How be I come help you for now? There's not a lot I can do out here." His eyes sought the area around the house and prayed for Micah's safety. It would be a very difficult area to search at night. He knew. He'd done it before.

Abe turned as his name was called and Matt jogged towards him. "No word yet, Abe?"

Abe shook his head, glancing at the darkening sky. "No, and I don't like it, Matt. It's not like Micah to disappear like this."

"No, it's not like any of us. Has anyone talked to Kataleen?"

Abe shrugged, not really sure. "I think Frankie was going to try and reach her." He looked back towards the compound. "Didn't we just go through this a while ago with one of you guys, searching up here?"

Matt gave a short bark of laughter. "We did. I was hoping we never had to go through that again."

Abe shook his head, then turned as one of the search and rescue officers headed down towards him.

"Abe, we've picked up a trail and we're running it now. If you want to follow me, I'll take you to where the dog made the hit."

Abe and Matt followed, prayers rising that they would find Micah. A shout from up ahead of them forced them into as fast a pace as they could get.

Matt pushed past the men standing near a large rock formation, and dropped to his knees, reaching out a hand to touch the body. Micah and he was alive. His bonds had already been cut and tagged for evidence. Matt, the paramedic on Abe's team, assessed him, then sat back as Micah moved.

"Micah, can you hear me?"

Micah rolled over on his back, hand going to the back of his head. "Yeah, I can hear you, Matt. Help me sit up."

"Take it easy, Micah. You've had a pretty good clip on the head."

"I know. It hurts. Now help me up."

Matt pulled Micah to a sitting position and then assessed his head further. "Doesn't look like you'll need stitches, but we'll still want you seen."

"I know I will." Micah tried to stand, lost his balance, and then rose with Matt's help.

"Are you sure you're okay to walk out of here?" Abe did his own assessment.

"I'm sure." Matt rubbed at his eyes, trying to clear his vision.

"What happened, Micah?" Frankie stood behind Abe, watching.

"I really don't know. I'm up here walking, heading back to the yard, came around a corner, and there's this guy sitting there pointing a gun at me. Wearing a mask. Never said a word. Maybe thirty minutes later, someone came up behind me and that's about all I remember." Micah was puzzled. "I don't have any enemies, Abe. I'm not out there on the front lines like the rest of you. I'm the one in the van keeping you all connected and feeding you information. It doesn't make sense."

"Not from your team point of view, Micah, but it does from Kat's point of view." Frankie's quiet words stopped their forward progress.

"What do you mean, Frankie?" Abe asked the question they all wanted to.

"Let's get Micah back down to the yard, and then we'll talk."

Eddie watched from his post in the kitchen doorway at Matt cleaned, then dressed Micah's wound. Micah refused to go to the Emergency, shrugging off their concerns, stating he would go later if he had to.

Micah's eyes never left Frankie's face. When Matt had finished and tucked away the supplies, Micah spoke.

"What aren't you telling me, Frankie? I know there's something."

Frankie shared a look with Eddie, then sighed, pulling out his phone. "I know already you're not going to like this, Micah. Kat received a card in the mail today, a "sweetheart" card. In it was a picture of you two." Frankie pulled up a photo on his phone and handed it over. Without releasing it, he spoke, eyes on Micah, "She has no idea who would have sent it, but she was scared enough to bring it right to me."

Micah frowned, then taking Frankie's phone, stared at the picture, his eyes shooting back up to him. "That was the other night. He's following her?"

Frankie nodded. "It looks that way. We're making arrangements for her office and classroom at the college. Joseph's finished with the security update? That's what I thought. Kat is going back over her consultations from the ancestry point of view. I have detectives contacting the police forces she's worked with as well as her home town force. This is very concerning, Micah, considering what happened to you."

Micah nodded, his mind turning over everything he knew. "She's okay?"

"She's fine, Micah. She was out here a while ago looking for you, then left before you were found." Eddie watched Micah's reaction, seeing the little that he gave away. Eddie nodded. Another one, Lord. Please help us keep them safe.

Micah nodded, glad she was okay but desperate to talk with her. He knew that wouldn't be happening. Matt would be staying very close, he knew, to keep an eye on him.

Chapter 8

Sunday morning, Micah stood at the back of the church, trying to decide where to sit. He really didn't want to be there, he wanted to find Kat instead. He had tried to reach her but had only gotten her voice mail, and she hadn't called him back. He finally gave up on where to sit and sat in one of the chairs at the back.

He looked up as someone spoke his name, then rose to his feet. Kat stood in front of him, concern on her face.

"Micah, how are you?"

He shrugged, then pointed at the chair beside his. She sank down, her eyes on him.

"I've been trying to reach you." His eyes on her face, he saw when she flushed and then reached for her phone.

"I set it to vibrate the other day when I was in a meeting. I always forget to take it off vibrate if I'm deep in thought." She looked at it, then at him. "I'm sorry, Micah. I would have called you back."

He nodded, then spoke. "Given what's going on, it's not a good idea to turn your phone to vibrate and forget about it."

She sighed. "You're right. I'm negligent that way. I see you called a few times."

He grinned. "I did, then I stopped, not sure if I should be calling you."

"It's okay if you do." She scrolled through the rest of the missed calls and messages and breathed a sigh of relief. "None from him in the last few days."

"He thinks he's made a point."

At the end of the service, Micah stood, staring around at the congregation. Something felt off, as if they were being watched, but he couldn't see anyone he didn't know. This was strange. He brought his mind back to the lady beside him as she spoke.

"Are you up to going to the picnic today, Micah?" She searched his face.

"I am. There's nothing wrong with me." He grinned. "Are you asking me to go with you?"

She stopped, staring at him, then started laughing. "I guess I am, seeing as I put it that way. So, will you?"

"Sure. I caught a ride in with Luke today. Are you driving?" He laughed as she shook her head at him, then headed to find Luke and Abigail, Luke's fiancée. He knew Luke wouldn't mind not having to give him a lift.

Sitting back on the grass at the river, Micah looked around. Leah and Joseph had joined for their lunch and now sat quietly talking. Kat had been persuaded to go for a walk with Greg's young daughter, Anna, who adored her cousin, it was obvious to all around.

A child's sudden screams and calls had all the men on their feet, looking around. Greg, recognizing his daughter's voice, ran for the trail Kat and Anna had taken.

"Daddy! Daddy! Help! He's going to hurt Kat. Help her, please Daddy!"

Greg swung his daughter into his arms and looked up the trail. Some of Abe's men were already half way up it as were some of the officers in attendance. Micah headed that way, then stopped as he heard a scream, then a splash of water. He headed for the river instead, a bad feeling inside. Kat! She's in the river. Emptying his pockets and shoving the contents into Leah's hands, he waded into the river. Searching upriver, he saw Kat. She was moving downstream with the river flow, but she wasn't moving herself. He dove into the water and began swimming towards where he had last seen her. A splash beside him and he heard Matt's voice calling to him.

Micah dove underwater, desperately seeking to find Kat. Above water, he shook his head and searched, heading back underwater. He saw her finally and swam rapidly towards her, hooking an arm around her and pulling her to the surface. Cradling her against his chest, he hit a stroke he hoped would get them to shore quickly.

Matt was there beside him as they carefully carried her to a blanket placed on the grass, cradling her head and neck. Matt dropped to his knees and listened.

"She's not breathing, Micah. Hurry. We need to work fast."

The two men worked rapidly. Finally, Micah heard a small breath and sat back. By that time, the town paramedics were there and took over, one of them looking up at Matt's question and shaking his head.

Matt looked at Micah, then up at Greg standing behind him. He rose and walked over to Greg.

"She's breathing on her own, Greg. Micah got to her in time. The paramedics are rushing her in. Go with them."

Greg nodded, then followed after the stretcher. Matt turned to Micah, draping the blanket he had been handed over his shoulders.

"Come on, Micah. Let's get you to Emerge too and get you checked out. That dunking after your head injury the other night needs assessing."

Micah slowly nodded, then turned to take his belongings from Leah. Compassionate eyes watched as he moved away, then turned to the ambulance drawing away. This was not how the picnic was to end.

Frankie approached Abe as he stood staring at the river. "It wasn't an accident, Abe. Someone pushed her."

Abe nodded. "That's what I thought when I heard Anna. I'm glad she didn't see it happen. Any evidence up there?"

"Not a whole lot. I'm getting tired of this, Abe. Every time we turn around, someone is getting hurt, and it's usually one of your team or their ladies. Will you stop already?" Spoken half in jest, Frankie was adamant he wanted this to stop.

Abe gave a snort of laughter. "If I could do that, I would, you know, Frankie. Any idea on who or why?"

Frankie shook his head. "No, and that's frustrating. She's been going over her records. We've pulled records from previous threats. There's nothing there."

"Then, if it's not there, it has to be here. Who would want her gone from here?"

Frankie stared at Abe. "Now, why didn't we think of that?"

Abe shrugged. "You would have at some point. Let me know if we can help in any way."

"I will. I've also passed the information on to Tracker's." Frankie watched as Abe walked towards his truck, knowing he was headed for the hospital, then turned as an officer approached him.

Dr. John Thompson, Emergency physician and friend, found Greg in the waiting room and hesitated before he approached him. Sitting down beside him, he leaned back, not speaking for a moment.

"If you're not talking, it's either good or bad, John."

John smiled at his pastor's comments. "It's not bad, Greg. I understand she's made you medical power of attorney for now." At Greg's nod, John continued, "So, here's the update. She battered and bruised from the fall and the rocks in the river. We have her on a ventilator at present because her oxygen levels are not where they should be when she's breathing room air. That should only be for the next few hours."

"God was good, then, sparing her worse injuries."

"That He was, Greg. She'll be moved to a room shortly and then you can see her." He looked past him at Micah sitting a couple of chairs away. "How's Micah?"

Greg shot him a glance. "I wish he would let you look at him. He was the one who found her today. A couple of days ago, he was knocked unconscious and left bound in the rocks around Abe's. He refused to see anyone for that."

John nodded, then stood. "I'll take him back and check him out. Is he interested in Kat?"

Greg smiled at that. "To put it mildly, I would say yes."

"Then get him in to see her at some point before he goes home. Kat will likely be in for at least overnight, if not tomorrow as well."

"You'll have a fight on your hands over that, John, if I know Kat."

Greg watched as John stopped by Micah, then hauled him to his feet and hand on his shoulder, moved him to an exam room.

Micah nodded when John finished his examination. He knew what he was going to say and slid off the examination bed.

"I'll be fine, John. It's not the first time for me to have a knock on the head, or a swim in cold water."

John nodded, assessing Micah as he spoke. "I know it's not. Just make sure you can get lots of rest in the next few days." John paused, then spoke again. "I'm butting in likely where I shouldn't. Greg's going to be with Kat. You can go up if you want."

Micah's eyes shot to John, a puzzled look on his face. "How is she?"

"Considering how far she fell and what she went through in the river, doing surprisingly well. I told Greg she'd be on a ventilator for a bit, but that's normal. Head on up. Here's her room number."

Greg stood at the foot of his cousin's bed, watching as she slept, the sounds of the machines filling the air around him. His heart lifted in prayer, knowing how her parents wanted to be there for her. He turned as he heard a tap at the door and looked behind him. Micah stood framed in the doorway, one hand holding the door open. He entered, not sure if he should be there.

Micah moved forward, eyes on Kat. He had only known her for a short while, but it seemed as if they had known each other for years.

"How is she, Greg?"

"Doing okay. They're planning on pulling the ventilator soon, if she can keep her oxygen levels up. How are you?"

Micah shrugged, not answering.

"Thank you, Micah. If you and Matt hadn't gone in so quickly, we wouldn't be standing here."

Micah shook his head. "Others were there, ready to go in."

Greg stared at him, then turned to the door.

"Listen, I need to run home and check on Anna, make sure she's okay. Can you stay with Kat for a while, just until I get back?"

Micah nodded. "I can. Abe's not coming back for a while, he said."

Greg hesitated, then spoke once more. "I know you don't want thanks, Micah. Kat's told me what's going on, what you and your team and Mac have done so far. I know Kat's never been interested in anyone, at least not since high school. There's a different tone in her voice when she speaks of you."

Micah had fixed his eyes on Greg as he spoke. "There is? She's a special lady, Greg. I won't hurt her."

Greg placed his hand on Micah's shoulder. "I know you won't. Whatever it is that's going on with her, I pray that it's resolved quickly, and then you two can explore this new fascination you seem to have with one another."

Micah looked over at him in shock as he laughed softly, then left. Micah stared after him for a few minutes, then found a chair to draw closer to the bed. He was chilled but that didn't seem to matter. All that mattered was the lady lying there in that bed.

A nurse, in on her rounds, saw the shivers still running through Micah's body and found a heated sheet to wrap him in. The warmth felt good, he thought, then fatigue weighed his eyelids down, and he slept.

Kat stirred, unsure where she was. Her throat hurt as did her whole body. Moving restlessly, she stared around. A hospital room? Now why? Turning her head, she caught a glimpse of a man sitting her bed, and her frown smoothed out as a softened expression crossed her face. Micah! What was he doing here?

She moved her hand slightly, and Micah stirred, blinking as he roused. His head tilted, and he smiled at her.

"How are you?"

"I'm okay. Why are you here?" Her voice was rough and barely above a whisper.

"Greg asked me to stay while he ran home for a bit. That was hours ago, though."

"Anna!"

"He wanted to make sure she was okay." Micah shot a glance at the door, then back at her. "Frankie's been around, wanting to talk with you. He said he'd be back. What happened?"

Kat shook her head. "I don't remember. I can remember us talking after church, and then nothing until now." She looked concerned, frowning at him.

"That's not unusual, I understand, not to remember things." Micah looked towards the door as it opened, and Frankie peeked in. "Evening, Frankie."

"Micah." Frankie approached the bed, studying the young woman lying there. He nodded. She looked rough but was finally awake. "I just need to ask you some questions, Kat."

"Ask away, but I can tell you, I don't remember anything after leaving the church until a few minutes ago." She watched him, her eyelids heavy with fatigue. "And if this can wait, I would like it to, please." Her eyes closed as she drifted off to sleep.

Frankie stared at her, dumbfounded. Then he looked at Micah. Micah was having a difficult time suppressing his laughter. Frankie's eyes narrowed, then he shrugged.

"Maybe tomorrow, she'll remember something. Abe's waiting outside for you.

I've posted an officer outside her door for the night."

Micah rose from his chair, carefully folding the blanket he had wrapped himself in, and then taking a last look at Kat, headed for the door after Frankie. Please, Lord, keep her safe overnight. Heal her.

Chapter 9

Micah stared at his laundry hamper. He needed to do his laundry, but it just wasn't happening. He paced back to the kitchen and poured a cup of coffee, moving to stare out the back door. No, the grass didn't need cutting, so he couldn't use that as an excuse. He wandered through to stare out the front window, then, heaving a sigh, detoured back through the kitchen to leave his mug on the counter on the way back to the laundry.

Sorting his laundry, he started the first load and then grabbed his shirts. Checking pockets was a matter of course for him. Finding the shirt he had been wearing the day he was attacked, he checked it for stains, then felt the pocket. He stopped, not remembering putting anything in a pocket that day. He slowly pulled out a folded piece of paper. Looking around, he still hesitated to unfold it. Was it a warning to him or to Abe, he thought?

Finally, he turned to the kitchen, laying the paper on the counter, and staring at it. Slowly unfolding it, he read it, then read it again, his head raising as he finished,

It wasn't Kat, it was Abe. Now it made more sense.

He read it again and turned, heading to shut off the washer and then find Abe and then to town to find Frankie.

"Abe!" Micah's shout caught him as he headed for his home, his work day done. He turned and watched as Micah ran towards him.

"Micah? What's the hurry?" Abe didn't the look on Micah's face.

"This!" Micah thrust the note at him. "I found this in my shirt pocket from the other day. That was about you, not Kat!"

Abe shot him a startled look, then took the proffered sheet. His face blanched as he read it.

Micah, watching his friend's face, saw the stern lines settle into it as he realized the implications.

"You're heading to find Frankie?"

"I am. You coming?"

Abe sighed. "I have to or else he'll track me down. I just wish I knew what this guy wanted. Maybe it would have saved you guys all this."

Heading for a break, Frankie had just walked away from the department building when he heard his name called. Stopping to look back, he found Micah and Abe almost upon him.

"You look like you mean business, guys." He waited as the two shared a look.

"We do but it looks as if we caught you at a bad time." Abe was still hesitant to talk to Frankie.

"Just heading to Mac's for a break. You may as well come along."

Once seated, Frankie again stared at the two men.

"Which one of you want to spill it."

Micah shot a look at Abe, then pulled a piece of paper from his pocket.

"I found this in the shirt pocket I was wearing the other night, Frankie."

Frankie took the paper with a sight. "So, you're telling me that was about Abe?"

He frowned as he read it. "Is this guy for real?"

"Tsk! Tsk! Tsk! Finlay, it's now at seven. You're next! You'll never know when or how."

"And you have no idea, Abe?" Frankie watched his friend closely.

"No, and I wish I did. I'd end it right here and now if I did." Abe's mind drifted away over the past years and stopped on a name, then he shook his head. That name was just too bizarre to even consider.

"You thought of someone?" Frankie had seen the fleeting look cross his face.

"Not really. That name is so far in the past, I couldn't even consider it. Another lifetime it was."

Frankie nodded, not sure that Abe was right. "If you do decide you want to share, you know where to find me." He stood and stared down at the two men. "Be very careful, you two. We have no idea of who we're dealing with."

Micah stood to leave as well, standing for a moment to stare down at Abe. "Are you okay, Abe?"

Abe looked up from his mug he had been studying and nodded. "I'm fine, Micah. Go find your lady, okay?"

Micah hesitated a moment, then turned to walk away, his thoughts on Abe. Something was going on there, he thought, but he wasn't sure how to broach the subject or if he even should. He finally shook his head, then stood staring around the parking lot, feeling someone's eyes on him. He couldn't see anyone, but someone was there. Now, he knew what the other guys had meant.

Kat looked up from her studies as she heard the doorbell ring. She wasn't expecting anyone, she thought. She took a look at her work, then sighed as the doorbell rang again. Whoever it was, they were persistent. Peeking through the window at the side of the door, her thoughts changed. Yes, this man was persistent, all right, but that's was okay in her books.

Unlocking the door and opening it, she stood staring at the tall man framed in her doorway, a smile of delight on her face.

"Micah! What are you doing here?"

He turned and grinned. "I wanted to see how you were feeling after your dunking."

"Come in." She closed the door behind him and pointed to the kitchen. "I really needed a break about now. What can I get for you?"

"Doesn't matter." Micah waited for Kat to decide what she wanted, watching as she stared into the open fridge. "Kat, what's in there you don't want?"

She smiled at his taunt. "Healthy stuff, Micah." She finally grabbed a bottle of juice for herself and water for him. She turned, studying him. "Why did you really come, Micah?"

He shrugged. "Found out, huh?" At her nod and smile, he said, "I wanted to spend some time with you, but it sounds as if I've caught you at a bad time."

She shook her head. "No, I was just doing some studying that I really didn't need to do. Other than that, I have some charities to decide on for the trust fund." At his look, she continued, "When I did the copyright on my family tree program, I set up a trust that gets all the royalties. I have a set point that once it goes over that, I have to put them overage into a charity."

"And it's a lot."

She nodded, not meeting his eyes, suddenly shy about the value of the trust.

Micah walked over to where she stood, moved her juice to the counter, and drew her into a hug. "Is it that much, sweetheart?"

He felt her nod against his chest. "It is. It's like a million or more right now, and I just can't figure out who to give it to."

He continued to rub her back, his thoughts racing. "So, this trust is worth a lot, then, is it? Do you need some help trying to come up with some charities?"

He felt her relax against him at that point. He knew then she had been waiting for him to draw away and reject her. That wasn't happening. "I could use some help. Brock has helped some in the past, but even my family doesn't know how much this is worth."

Micah knew this was a crucial point in their relationship. If he failed, he would lose this lady. Lord, I could use Your help right now to help this lady. Where can she put this money to get Your truth out there?

"Okay, so how about we head for your office and decide what you want to do? You can walk me through the process of what you usually do."

Micah found himself the recipient of a sudden hard hug, then her arms dropped as she pulled away to head for her office.

Kat drew a big breath. Micah had responded differently than anyone else who had known of the trust fund, and there were not a lot who did.

Micah finally looked up from the paperwork he had been reading and watched Kat as she struggled to come to decisions about the money.

"Kat, stop for a minute. Do you need to do this today or is there a time frame we can work with?"

She looked up, blinked, then focused on him. "You're right. I don't need to do this today. I have about two months, but I usually do it right away so it's not hanging over my head."

"So, why don't we set this aside for now? You need a break. I need a break. Let's go get something to eat or at least a coffee?"

She looked at him and smiled. "That sounds like a plan."

Four weeks later, Micah looked at the lady sitting beside him in church. She had become a huge part of his life in the last few weeks, even though they were no closer to finding her stalker. She looked up at him then and smiled, her attention going back to her cousin. He too looked forward, but his mind was not on the sermon until he caught a phrase and then he listened.

Greg watched with amusement as Kat and Micah circled around to leave. He knew Kat was avoiding him, and he also knew he would catch up with her soon. He raised his eyes as he felt evil in the house. He frowned as he stared around. Who was it, Lord? Is it directed at our Kat?

Micah looked behind him as they walked towards his truck. Someone was there, he knew. He just wished he could find whoever it was.

Chapter 10

Abe turned to watch as his team made their way across the parking lot at the compound. It had been a busy week for them, learning new techniques themselves so they could teach others. And tomorrow, they would be sitting through a seminar given by Kat. He wasn't sure on that himself but had decided they all needed to hear what she had to say. Micah would just laugh when questioned on what they would face.

Kat looked up the next morning and scanned the participants in her seminar. Bob was to have been there, but his heart attack the day before meant she was on her own. She had done it before and could do it again, but given the threat against her, she just wasn't sure if she was up to it. Her eyes stopped and narrowed. Don't tell me, she thought. Abe really did follow through on his threat to bring his whole team. And I can safely say Micah wouldn't tell them want they were facing. She smiled. Okay, let's get this show on the road, and buckle up, everyone.

"Good morning. Welcome to all of you. I know most of you have no idea what to expect and likely don't even want to be here, but your powers to be have decided otherwise.

"My name's Kataleen Evans. I developed this program and this course. First, a bit about me."

She clicked up a bit of film of a vehicle racing around road cones. "This is what I used to do for a living, until I moved here. This is a course designed by my family to teach drivers how to handle icy conditions. In this case, we're out on a lake, four feet of ice beneath us, and I'm doing 45 or 50 at this point." She clicked to the next picture. "This is what we do for fun where I come from. It's called mudding, and the muddier you come home, the better the day's been." She had brought up a picture of a very muddy truck. "Oh, just in case you're interested, it was my aunt who taught me all about mudding. And if you happen to attend Greg Evans' church back in Riverville at some point, ask him about his mom's mudding experiences. Let's just say, females rule!" Laughter spread through the room.

"Now, on to the family tree and crime. How does it fit you say? Fasten your seatbelts, ladies and gentlemen. You're about to experience what driving on ice is like without once leaving this room."

With that, the course was underway. Abe watched as Kat interacted and drew everyone into the discussion, whether they really wanted to or not. She had an ability to do that he had never seen before. He took a look around at his fellow team members and saw how rapt their attention was. Good, he thought. Now we'll be able to have a reasonable discussion on this and how it fits with our work.

"And that's that, ladies and gentlemen. Thank you for your participation today. I have all your contact information and your certificates will be headed your way. Any questions, my contact information is on the back sheet. Bob's is there as well but he is seriously ill right now, so please don't contact him."

Watching as she chatted with the participants as they left, Micah turned as Abe approached. "Didn't expect that, did you?" he asked with a grin.

Abe shook his head. "Absolutely not. She's good." He looked around. "We're heading over to the restaurant. Joseph's waiting for you two."

Micah nodded, knowing they needed someone else with them. "No problem. We should be along shortly."

Micah headed Kat's way as she raised her head to look for him. After a few more words, she excused herself to find him in her way. Reaching out, he pulled her into a hug.

"You did great."

"Thank you. Abe impressed?"

Micah started to laugh as he reached to take her briefcase and then her hand, heading towards Joseph. "Yes, he was."

Late the next week, Micah tracked Frankie down. "Anything new, Frankie?"

Frankie turned as Micah approached him. "With Kat? No, not a thing. Has she had any more messages?"

"Not that I've heard, and she promised to tell me."

"We're at a loss here, Micah, unless we can get an idea of who or why."

Micah nodded. "I know. That worries me, Frankie, that we won't figure it out in time. Those messages are escalating."

At that point, Frankie looked up to see Kat standing at the front counter. "Your lady's here, Micah."

Micah spun, then waited as Frankie went to meet her. As she neared him, he saw the distress on her face and his heart sank. *She's got another text or message, hasn't she, Lord? Please help us find the guy and get to the truth of it all.*

Kat walked straight into Micah's arms and hugged him as tight as she could. "I was praying I would find you, but I didn't expect to find you right here."

"God knew. Now, let's follow Frankie, and you can tell him what's going on."

Seated in Frankie's office, Kat hesitated, her eyes on the floor.

"Kat?" Micah's voice had a question. "Kat, what did you get?"

She raised her eyes to Frankie. "I want this to stop, Frankie. I don't know how or who, but I'm done." She handed over her phone and then a package they hadn't seen in her hands. "I haven't opened the package, but it has to be from him."

Frankie nodded, then turned to the message she had scrolled to. "When did you do your last seminar?"

"Last weekend. Micah was there as were all of Abe's men."

"Whoever this is was there, in the room."

She nodded as Micah's eyes flew between Frankie and her.

"In the room?"

Frankie nodded and handed over the phone. Micah could feel the anger building and had to work to tamp it down. A clear picture of Kat from that day was on the screen, with the words, *"You were warned"* scrawled across it.

Micah studied it, then looked at Kat. "No, that's the angle where Abe's guys were sitting. I think……" He paused, running scenarios through his mind. "Frankie, can you get someone to check that room for a camera from that angle? It looks as if it's been taken from behind where we were sitting and then cropped."

Frankie reached for the phone again. "I think you're right, Micah." He reached for his phone to set that in motion.

"Now for the package. You haven't opened it?"

Kat shook her head. "No, I haven't. I didn't want to. I'm not even sure if I want to know what's in it."

Frankie reached for a pair of scissors, then stopped. He reached for his phone instead and asked for a crime scene tech to come to his office.

They watched as the tech took photos of the package and then worked to open it. Once the box was open, the tech stopped, threw a questioning glance at the two civilians sitting there, then said something low to Frankie.

Frankie nodded as the tech left, thoughts running rampant at what was in the box. He looked up to find both Micah and Kat staring at him.

"You really have no idea who it is, Kat?"

She shook her head. "If I did, I would confront them and end this."

"That would not be a good idea, Kat, confronting them." He looked down into the box again. "Micah, did you see anyone odd that day at the seminar?"

"None of us did, and we were watching."

Frankie nodded. "Then, what's in the box is totally bizarre to what's going on. We have a picture of you two with Joseph near your truck, Micah. We have bunch of dead daisies with tiny blue flowers as well. We also have a sympathy card.'

Kat drew in a breath, then reached for Micah's hand. "A sympathy card?"

Frankie nodded again as he flipped the card open. "A sympathy card, addressed to your parents."

Kat began shaking her head. "Who would do that? They know nothing about the seminar or what I do."

Micah stood and approached Frankie. "Can I see the photo?" He studied it as Frankie held it for him. "Kat, that's just as we were leaving. I can remember feeling someone watching us, and Joseph mentioned it."

"I don't remember that feeling." She sank back in her chair. "I guess I won't be giving any more seminars for now, then. It's putting everyone around me at risk."

She rose and also approached Frankie. "You said small blue flowers?" She peeked around Micah into the box, a puzzled look on her face. "Forget-me-nots." She was still, then the two men could hear her saying very quietly, "He loves me, he loves me not, forget me not." Her eyes raised, she stared into the distance. "Quite the combination of flowers. I've heard that combination somewhere. I just can't remember."

She turned and walked out of Frankie's office, leaving the two men staring after her. Micah went after her and brought her back.

"Talk to us, Kat. What's going on in that mind of yours?"

She shook her head as she looked between the two men. "I'm not sure yet. But this is going to stop." This time, she was gone before Micah could stop her.

"What's she up to, Micah?"

Micah shook his head. He had spent enough time with Kat to know she wasn't going to stand for any more. "I don't know, Frankie, but I can tell you, she's getting ready to go on the offensive."

"We don't need that, Micah. Can you stop her?"

Micah stared at Frankie, then started to laugh. "Not likely, Frankie. She's one determined lady when she makes up her mind."

“Can you at least try?”

“I will but I don’t think it will work.” Micah headed out of the building, intent on finding his lady.

Chapter 10

Turning back to the door as Kat opened it, Micah studied the face of the woman he had come to love. It was showing the strain of what she was going through, and he wanted to take that burden from her. He entered as she stood back, closing the door behind him. He watched her eyes and then reached to draw her close to his heart.

They spoke for a while, then Kat went to find a jacket and her purse. She was not totally convinced that the route they had chosen to take would work, but she knew she wanted this man in her life for a long time.

On the Thursday, Nathaniel watched as Micah and Kat headed for the conference room at the compound. Abe had called the team together, along with Kat, to see what they could do to move the investigation along. He knew that Frankie had talked to Abe, and it wasn't going anywhere from the police standpoint.

Settled around the table and the material Kat had provided in front of them, the team started reading.

"When did the text messages start, Kat?" Murphy picked up on that right away.

"About six and a half years ago, I think, Murphy. It was about eighteen months after I gave my first seminar. That was a disaster, hardly anyone there."

"Is there any way of finding the names of those who attended?" Joseph was trying to come up with a solution.

Kat shrugged. "Not likely at this point. I can go through my files and see if I have a list of names." She turned to study Joseph. "Even if I have the names, it may not lead us anywhere."

"No, but it's a start."

Abe had been reading ahead in the material. "Tell us about the program, Kat. You don't say a lot in what you've given us."

"No, I haven't. There's not a lot I can say, unfortunately." She sighed, then started to pace, Micah's eyes watching her. She looked up and he gave her an encouraging nod.

"Okay, so I'll explain what I can. The program I developed is very private. It's not out there for public use. It's only known by word of mouth. How it works is different. A person sends an email to a secure email, stating who they are and why they need to use the program. They have to go through a verification process. If accepted, then a questionnaire is emailed to them, asking for more information. This again has to go through a verification program. If they pass this step, then they are granted access to the program for 24 hours only, and only for the purpose in the original email. The program tailors itself to what they have provided. Once the 24 hours are up, they are locked out and can't access it any more.

"The program cannot be downloaded at all. If someone tries to hack into, they can only get so far and then they locked and blocked. If someone were to hack all the way, then the program starts to destroy itself within 45 seconds of them getting through. Once it's destroyed, that's it. There is no more program."

The men's eyes were on her. "How do they trace the program to you?"

Kat shook her head. "They can't. The program has been patented and copyrighted to a trust fund, and there are so many layers to the trust fund it would take months to work through them all. The original lawyers are no longer involved, they only helped set up the trust fund and the patent and copyright. The accountant firm is changed every two years and only one person at the firm has access to the financials, not to the actual program."

"That's an interesting way to have it set up, Kat." Ian, the paralegal on the team, studied his notes, and then looked up at her. "Who knew you were developing this program?"

She shook her head. "No one. I started working on it when I was about 15 and refined it about four years later. It took about two years for the legal process to work through and have it under the trust fund." She turned to walk over to Micah. "Just so you know, the program is very expensive and very limited as to availability. The trust is set up in such a way that it makes so much money, and anything over that goes to charities."

"What charities do you donate to?" Matt's question caught her off guard, and she spun to study him.

"It varies, Matt. No one charity gets something every month. I look at women and children's   shelters,   missing   children organization, scholarships, that kind of thing."

Matt nodded. "A wide variety."

Micah spoke up. "There is a wide variety and what Kat donates every three months is substantial. She does it in such a way that no one charity knows who the donor is."

Abe nodded as he listened. "So, it's not someone coming after you for the money, then. It has to be someone after the program."

Kat agreed. "It has to be. If it were to fall into the wrong hands, it would be deadly for law enforcement. I really hesitated about finishing it off. That's why I've set it to self-destruct. It can't be replicated. As I said, everyone who accesses it has a different version, based on the information they have provided and what they are looking for. We have tried to build in every safety feature we can think of."

She walked over to take a look at the papers Nathaniel had been reading. "It looks as if I got away with about eighteen months before the texts started."

Nathaniel stopped reading, his focus on her hand, as he spoke. "And the text messages only come when you've given a seminar."

Nathaniel reached to stop her hand, his attention on her ring finger. He looked up at her, a grin on his face, as she nodded. Shooting a quick look at Micah, he held up her hand, and the men were quick to pick up on what she was wearing. Micah had proposed earlier in the week and she now wore a rose quartz ring.

Kat bit back a giggle at the men stared at her, then at Micah, grins crossing their faces. She knew they were happy for them.

"Kat, did anyone ever ask you about the program?" Micah was still deep in thought, trying to fathom how word got out.

"No one, sweetheart." Kat's voice held a hidden smile.

"Sounds to me like you're up to no good." Micah had a small smile on his face. He had figured out what was going on behind his back.

"Not me, dearest, but I know some men who are surprised, stunned, shell shocked, shall we say?"

"Quite the run on "S" words there, my dear."

"Yes, it is. Shall I continue or switch letters?"

Micah just shook his head, his thoughts going back to what he had been reading. "Kat, this man who tried to claim you took his thoughts and didn't share the fame with him? Who is he?"

Kat walked back to behind his chair, reading over his shoulder. "I have no idea who that is. That's the first I've seen his name." She stopped, eyes focused in the distance. "I kept it so close to me that no one ever had a glimpse of anything. I have always had really good firewalls and security features in place. Not even my family is aware of the trust or what it involves."

Nathaniel looked up from his notes. "Why don't we pass that on to Trackers's?"

Micah turned in his chair to eye Nathaniel. "I think we should. How about you and I pay Jace a visit?"

"Sounds like a plan. But now, we want to know why you didn't share your news with us?" Nathaniel was up to no good, the rest of the team could tell, and they laughed.

"Because it's so brand new?" Micah ducked the paper balls flying his way. "We had planned to share today." He stood and reached to draw Kat to his side. He looked down at her as he spoke. "We realize we haven't known each other that long, but it's like God brought us together, just like He did with all of you." He bit his lip, not quite sure how to proceed.

Kat shook her head. "What Micah is trying to say is that we have decided not to wait. We're planning on getting married a week from Saturday. It's not much notice, but we're confident that God is working things out for us."

Surprised, the men stared at the two, then rose to congratulate them. Abe hugged Kat. When she stepped back, she was struck by a look in his eyes, and studied him. She then reached to hug him again.

"Whoever you gave your heart to, Abe, she still has it. Trust that God brings her back." Kat's voice was low enough that only Abe heard her.

Abe was stunned. What had she seen? She didn't know him, didn't know his history. He nodded, then stepped back to watch.

Just after lunch, Kat went to answer her door, surprised to see nine ladies standing her. She stood back, a smile on her face.

"I guess you heard, did you?"

"We did." Adriel spoke up. "We're here to help you seeing as your family is not close. Mary's here to represent them."

"So she is. Now, what are you ladies up to?"

"We need to know what you want us to do." Leah spoke up. "What plans have you come up with and where do we go with them for you?"

Kat looked around at the ladies standing in her hallway. "First, coffee needs to go on. I've some treats from the Irish Charm that need eating. I'll go find my notes and then we can get started. Micah warned me you would be around as soon as word got out."

Rebecca spoke up. "I've been through this twice, Kat. The first time with all the bells and whistles with my first husband. Then eloping with Gideon." Rebecca stopped for a minute, remembering how her first husband had been murdered just as they had been married for three months. "What we can do is help you plan something in-between that if you like."

Lydia spoke up. "Just don't talk to Ian. He'll want to help you run away and hide. He's offered to do that with all of us."

Kat stared at her, mouth open. "Not really!"

Heads were nodding. "All of us! Now lead us to the coffee and sweets, and we'll get started." Elizabeth headed for the kitchen.

Gathered in the living room, laughter and fun spilled through the afternoon. Finally, Leah spoke up.

"What about your dress, Kat? Have you chosen one yet?"

Kat nodded, blinking back tears. "Let me show you." She rose and headed for her bedroom, coming back with a garment bag in her hand. "It was my Mom's and she couriered it to me yesterday." She pulled the dress from the bag, and the other women oohed and aahed.

"Go, put it on, Kat. Then we can see if we need to help with anything." Mary smiled at Kat through her tears. She knew Greg wasn't happy with how quick Micah and Kat had decided to marry and had told Kat that.

Kat returned, dressed in the gown, a simple white dress, with beading and gathers, lace sleeves, and a sweetheart neckline. They decided nothing needed to be done with it.

"What about your hair?" Elizabeth asked.

"I'm wearing it down, with just held back at the sides with two combs that were my grandmother's. I don't like veils and I think that will work just as well."

Hours later, Kat tucked the dress back into the garment bag and hung it back in her closet, her thoughts on the day. She smiled, then turned as she heard her phone.

Paling, she read the message and then went searching for Frankie's card. This text message was not coming in sequence like it usually did. That meant whoever it was had been watching her.

Frankie read the message Kat had forwarded to him. It was too late that night to do anything, but he would be on it in the morning. He had heard from Abe that Micah and Kat were planning on marrying the next week, and he wanted to ensure that all was well.

Chapter 11

Micah and Nathaniel stepped into the reception area of a small business office and looked around. It looked comfortable but sparse.

"Can I help you?" A woman at the fax machine looked up at them.

"Yes. We're to meet with Jace. We're from Rebel's."

She nodded, then turned to an office. "Your people are here, Jace."

"Be right there, if I can get my program up."

"You need to either replace your hard drive or the complete tower. You've been told that for months now, Jace."

"I know, Tracker, but it's been so busy."

"Now's the time to do it. You can log in on mine while I'm away." Tracker walked to the front desk, and picking up the phone, called their local computer supply store, asking for a tower to be sent out the next day. "You know the one I got a month or two ago, Tony. That one or one similar or better. Jace needs one. Thanks." She turned around as Jace came to get Nathaniel and Micah. "Your new tower will be here tomorrow. Have it up and running by next week when I'm back."

Micah and Nathaniel watched with curiosity the looks flying between the two, then watched as Jace sighed and nodded. Following him to his office, they sat.

Jace took the material he was handed and scanned through it. "Really, this guy has been sending these messages?"

Micah nodded. "He has. Kat reported them when they first started but it was all just swept under the rug. Frankie is trying to get a handle on it but is at a loss."

Jace turned to his key board and soon his fingers were flying. He eventually stopped and stared at the monitor.

"Tracker, do you remember that case we had a few years ago? The one where the copyright of a computer program was at stake?"

Tracker appeared at his doorway. "I do. They never did catch the fellow, did they."

"No, I think he was gone before they got to him." He spun in his chair, staring at the two men sitting in front of him. "Didn't he have a whole slew of aliases?"

Tracker nodded. "He did." She disappeared, then returned with a file. "Here's most of them that we traced to him. I'm sure he's added more to that."

Micah and Nathaniel exchanged glances. "You've been after this fellow?"

Tracker stared at them, then nodded. "We have been. Every once in a while, we run through his aliases to see where he is. He's gone underground. But I must say, if he's after one of your ladies, keep her close. He's a nasty bit of work, tied to a few murders that no one could prove."

Micah stilled a shudder running through him. That was not what he wanted to hear, but exactly what he and Abe had discussed. "I don't like that."

"No, I wouldn't think you would. Jace, I'm off for the week. Catch me on my personal, I may or may not answer."

Jace spun to face the door, then shook his head. "That's that, then. She'll not answer. She'll be too busy flying with the eagles."

"So, where do we stand then, Jace?" Nathaniel's voice brought him back around.

"I'll keep running this. Maybe this time we can catch him. I hope so. He's tried too many times to claim other people's work as his, resulting in millions of dollars in law suits." He looked between the two men. "Whose lady is she?"

Micah spoke up. "She's mine. She developed a program in use by law enforcement, and she's been threatened to hand it over or die."

Jace shivered at the bite in Micah's voice. "We'll make sure we do our best so that doesn't happen. Who do I get the material to?"

"Frankie or Eddie, Nathaniel, and myself." Micah hesitated, then continued, "At least, until next Friday. Then I'm off the grid on my honeymoon for a week."

Jace studied him. "I can't promise to have anything before then, but we'll see what we can do."

Micah stood and shook Jace's hands. "Do your best as always, Jace. That's all we ask."

Nathaniel watched Micah as they crossed to his truck. He could tell Micah was worried but hiding it.

"You're worried, Micah," he commented as he pulled away from the business.

"I am, Nathaniel. I'm just afraid we won't find this guy in time. I don't know if I can handle losing Kat so soon, if something happens." Micah stared out the window at the passing scenery, not taking it in. "She got another text the other night. Frankie said there's nothing they can do without any more information. When they try and trace back, it comes back to a throwaway phone."

Nathaniel drew a deep breath. Lord, I'm out of my depth here. We need Your guidance and wisdom in this. How do we get to the truth of the matter, Lord, before something bad happens to Kat or Micah?

Kat turned as she heard her name called as she was crossing the college parking lot. Frankie was walking towards her. Has he news, Father, or just more of we don't know who it is and can't do anything?

"Frankie. What brings you here?" Kat studied his face.

Frankie pointed towards a bench near the parking lot. "Let's sit, okay? I've been on my feet all day and could use a moment or two off them."

Kat sat, watching closely. She saw the conflicting emotions Frankie was trying to hide. "Spit it out, Frankie. What did you chase me down to tell me?"

Frankie's eyes shot to her, and then he laughed. "Can't put anything past you, can I?" He drew a deep breath. "We're making some progress, Kat. That last text message, we were able to approximate where it came from for a change, in the downtown area. It doesn't look as if the phone was thrown away, and that's something new. He's been using the same number, just a different phone and carrier each time. This time, he's gone back to a previous carrier. Eddie's working on getting a court order to search the records."

"At least, we have some progress at last. I want this over, Frankie. If it means holding a press conference, without giving out much information, then that's what I'll do."

Frankie shook his head. "Not yet. If you hold a press conference, then you have to discuss the program, and I know you want that kept quiet.”

She sighed. “I do, but a program isn’t worth how I’m living.” She stopped, gathering her thoughts. “I am thinking I need to shut it down anyway. If God blesses Micah and I with children, I don’t want that hanging over their heads, or ours, not knowing if one of them would be kidnapped in order to get it.”

Frankie nodded. Kat had been doing some deep thinking. “What does Micah say?”

She shrugged. “He doesn’t want to see it shut down as it does so much good, but he agrees that we can’t put children at risk.” She sighed again. “I just don’t know, Frankie. I’ve tried to come up with a name for you, and I just can’t. Other than the name Micah landed on when we had that meeting with Abe’s team.”

“The one he passed on to Tracker? That man has an interesting history, to say the least. Jace is still working on that.” He sat back, studying the area around him, enjoying the warmth of the late autumn sun. “Are your plans all ready for Saturday?”

“They are. I am so glad you and Deirdre can make it.”

"Abe's been a good friend over the years. His team has too. We want to be there for you two."

Frankie stood. "Let me walk you to your car and then I have to run."

Micah stood as he saw Kat pulling into her driveway. He had been waiting for her. Tomorrow night was the rehearsal and then the next day, the wedding. Her family was in town and he knew she wanted to spend some time with them, but he just needed to see her without anyone else around.

Kat's face lit up when she saw Micah and she walked into his arms for his hug.

"This is nice, coming home to this." Kat laid her head on his chest, the thumping of his heart comforting to her.

"In two days, we'll do this for the rest of our lives, Kat. I still can't believe God has led me to you." He felt her nod. "Look, I know you want to spend tonight with your family. Go, get changed, and we'll go for a quick walk by the river on our way to the restaurant. I need some our time."

Kat leaned back to look up at him. "I'll be quick."

Micah looked around the table in the restaurant. His family was there, parents, brothers, Kat's parents, her parents and her brother and his wife. He listened to the talk and teasing, but underneath, he was worried. He was worried and yes scared that they wouldn't find the man responsible for the threats until it was too late. His prayer was that Frankie or Jace would come up with something over the next week, but he doubted that would happen.

Kat's father looked up at that point and caught the look on Micah's face and wondered at it. They hadn't gotten to know Micah very well but were satisfied with the man God had led their Kat to. His thoughts shifted to Greg and knew he would have to speak with his nephew. His antagonism towards the marriage was coming through, and Kat's Dad didn't understand it.

Kat's Dad tapped at Greg's office door the next morning. Greg looked up, pleased to see his uncle. After a few comments, her father paused.

"What is it with you, Greg? Why are you so against this marriage? Your attitude is coming through, and I don't understand it. If you don't change your attitude, I'm prepared to go find another minister. I won't have this special day of Kat's and Micah's ruined."

Greg sat back. It was not often his uncle spoke to him in such a manner. Then he felt ashamed. He was right. He had no real reason for his attitude, other than it was his cousin Kat getting married and he knew the danger of the work Micah was involved in.

"You're right, Uncle Andrew. I have no real reason for my attitude, other than it's Kat."

"See that you apologize to her and straighten it out. I know she wants you to perform the wedding, but I will take steps. Let's take some time for prayer, Greg. I would suspect you've been avoiding just that."

Greg nodded. "Pastor or not, sometimes our humanness comes through and we falter and fail. I'll make it up to her."

Chapter 12

Micah paced Greg's office, nerves showing, as his brother, Drew, watched, a smile on his face.

"She's not going anywhere, Micah."

Micah nodded. "I know she's not, Drew. I'm just worried about that fellow who's been sending her those text messages." Micah had had a long talk with Drew after the rehearsal the night before. Drew was a computer programmer and knew even better than Micah what the ramifications were.

"You'll get him. Sounds as if he's starting to get careless."

Micah turned to study his brother. "He is, but that doesn't mean much if we don't find him."

Greg popped his head into the office. "Come on, you two. We're ready for you now."

Micah's hands shook as he placed the wedding band on Kat's fingers, then looked up into her eyes. The calmness and peace there helped to steady him. If she had been nervous, it wasn't showing.

Finally on their way to a location they refused to tell anyone, Micah reached for Kat's hand. She turned her head to watch him, a smile on her face.

"What happened with Greg?" Micah's question was not what she had expected.

"Dad. He talked to him yesterday and told him to shape up or he'd find another minister."

"He didn't really, did he?" Micah was shocked.

Kat nodded. "Dad doesn't usually get involved, but when he does, we listen."

"And did he get involved when you told him you were getting married?" Micah shot her a glance. They hadn't really talked about their families.

Kat shook her head. "He's known of you for years and that Greg thinks highly of you. He asked some questions, then said nothing. If he had been concerned, he would have spoken up."

A week later, Micah backed his truck up to Kat's garage. They were planning on staying there that night as Kat wanted to pack up her office and move it out to Micah's home. He put his hand on her arm.

"Stay put until I come around." He headed to unlock and open the house door, then came back to open the truck door. He gathered Kat into his arms and carried her into the house, setting her on her feet and claiming a kiss.

Kat was laughing. "You don't plan on doing that tomorrow, do you?"

At his grin and nod, she shook her head. "You're crazy, you know that?"

"Crazy in love with my wife. Now, where do we start?" He watched as she nibbled at her lower lip.

"I guess the office, Micah. I'll need what's there. If you want to start there, I'll start on my clothes." She turned back. "What about supper? The fridge and freezer are empty, you know."

"I'll just call Mac's and have him send us something. Knowing Mac, he'll deliver it himself."

"Even to a tenant he's losing?"

Micah tilted his head to study her, sensing her uncertainty. "Even to her. He's not mad at you; in fact, he's very happy for us. He'll want to meet the new Mrs. O'Connor and welcome her into his family."

Kat stared at him. "His family? He must have a huge one by now."

"He does. It just keeps growing."

The watcher stood in place, eyes on the house. He saw the truck pull up and the two enter the house. He waited for the truck to leave, finally leaving himself. Back early in the morning, he saw the truck still there. What was going on, he thought? She never has a man stay overnight.

Then he turned to the newspaper he held. He turned to the classifieds and saw the announcement. How dare she, he thought? How dare she get married and go on with her life, leaving him destitute and without that program, the idea he was sure she had stolen from him? She would pay in a way she never thought possible.

Luke watched as Micah gathered up some boxes and headed for his cabin, then walked over and grabbed some as well.

"Micah!" he called, causing Micah to stop and turn around.

"Luke, you don't have to do that, you know."

"I know." Luke shrugged. "I just thought you could use some help."

"It's appreciated. They go into the spare room. Kat's setting it up as her office. I still have to go get her desk and chairs."

"I'll go with you. You'll need some help."

"How were things around here last week?"

"Quiet. Paul Adams stepped in when we needed an extra instructor. It's too bad he took that hit all those years ago. He really misses working in security."

"I know it wasn't with our team it happened, but it still hurts to see a friend injured like that. I'm glad he can still pick up for Abe now and then, when one of us has to be away for a period of time."

Luke nodded. "He picked up for me a while ago, when Matt and Sarah went through what they did. Abe has a line on a security team that could use his expertise. He's put him in touch with them."

"Well, hello, Luke. Been put to work, I see?" Kat's laughing voice caused Luke to turn from where he had set down the boxes.

"Welcome back, Mrs. O'Connor." Luke dropped a kiss on her cheek. "I'm off to help Micah with your desk and furniture."

"Oh, that's so sweet. Thank you."

"What all do you want from the house today, Kat?" Micah wrapped his arms around his wife.

"The desk, desk chair, the armchairs, and if possible, the book cases? That sounds like so much, but it's all that's in the office."

"Do you want anything else from there before next week?"

She shook her head. "No, I don't think so. Mac told me to take what time I needed to clear the house. We have to sort through what we both want to keep."

Later that afternoon, Micah headed for the office to see what work waited him there. Abe found him there after about an hour.

"Micah, welcome home."

Micah spun in his chair at Abe's voice. "Thanks, Abe. I don't see a lot piled up here."

"No, we managed to keep on top of it for you. We're having to head out in about 10 days for an overnight assignment. Just a quick in and out, I pray."

Micah nodded. "I see that on the schedule. Any word on our guy?"

Abe shook his head. "Not yet." He looked around. "A patrol officer was by Kat's place this morning and saw that the area was disturbed and found a crumpled newspaper lying there."

"What aren't you telling me, Abe?" Micah knew Abe well enough to know he was holding something back.

Abe stared at Micah, then looked past him before looking back at him. "It was turned to your wedding announcement. Frankie thinks this is going to set him off."

Micah sighed. "We talked about that when we were deciding whether to place an announcement. Kat wants this over, and so do I. This is part of the plan to flush him out."

Abe nodded. "That's what the guys figured. How do we keep you two safe, though, that is the question?"

"I'll talk to Kat and see what she has to say."

Micah rolled over in bed sometime during that night and realized Kat wasn't there. He raised up and saw light coming from her office. He rose and went to find her.

Kat looked up as he sank to the floor beside her. "What's wrong, sweetheart?"

She looked up from the pictures she had been sorting through, tears in her eyes. "He was there, Micah, he had to have been. At the very first seminar." She held out a picture to him. "There is only one person I can track back that wasn't law enforcement. He gave credentials as an investigator. I think if Frankie or Jace track him back, he's neither."

"Which one?"

She pointed to a man standing at the end of a row, not really seeming to want to be in the picture. "I don't know who took the picture now, but they wanted it for publicity. My lawyers confiscated all the photos and threatened to sue if any showed up at all."

"We'll need to get this to both Frankie and Jace." He reached to wrap her in his arms. "What made you remember that tonight?"

She shrugged. "I don't know. Something we were talking about last night, I suppose." She turned to look at him. "Will this end it, do you think?"

"I pray it does but be prepared that it doesn't. We need to figure out how to keep you safe on your drive back and forth." He laid his chin on her hair. "Abe told me that the team's going to be away overnight in about 10 days. How do I go with this hanging over our heads?"

"You go with God, Micah, and pray that we stay safe. If something happens, then we know God's still there and in control. Isn't it Murphy who is always telling you God has a plan for us and we don't know what it is?" At his nod, she continued, "I know that someday the real and whole truth about what is going on will come out. Until then, I just leave my hand in His and walk the course He has set."

"And that's so hard to do. Are you sure you're not a preacher?"

She laughed, then stood. "It's almost morning, sweetheart. I'm going to put on some coffee." She stopped and looked down at him. "You realize that this is our first Sunday in our church as Mr. and Mrs.?"

He grinned as he stood and claimed a kiss. "I do. I'm sure your cousin will have something to say about that."

"Unfortunately, I think he will."

Chapter 13

Two weeks later, Nathaniel and Micah once more sat in Jace's office, waiting for him to come back. They could hear low conversation at the back of the office building, then Jace appeared.

"Sorry, guys. I was running something by Tracker." Jace sat down, then reached for a folder. "This is what we have on your guy, Micah. That picture was really helpful, by the way."

"Kat hoped it would be." Micah looked over at the door as Tracker appeared and leaned against the door frame. "What did you learn about him?"

"He's the guy we've been trying to track down for years. We have never been able to find a picture of him until now."

Tracker spoke up, holding the sucker she had had in her mouth in her hand. "That was a really nice piece of work on her part. Keeping that picture just might keep her alive."

Jace turned to glare at her. "Another sucker, Tracker?"

She stared at it, then at him. "Stop knocking my veggies, Jace."

"Sugar is not a veggie, Tracker. We've had this discussion before."

"Sure, it is. Sugar comes from sugar cane, which is a plant, and plants are veggies. Therefore, my suckers are veggies. And the same goes for my chocolate."

Nathaniel and Micah stared at the two, then started to laugh. Micah caught the wink Tracker sent his way. Lightening the atmosphere, he thought. Good move, Tracker. This helps.

Jace turned, grumbling under his breath. "So, about this guy. We know he's here in town somewhere, but just where we're not sure. I've passed this on to Frankie, and he's working that angle." He stared at the two men seated across from him. "You know, this keeps it from going to a cold case. If this has been the guy all along, why hasn't he acted before?"

"How do we find him?" Nathaniel spoke up.

"I'm not sure that we can." Tracker moved over to Jace's desk, turning the list of names towards her. Micah watched as her finger traced down them. Then his attention was caught by the wedding band she wore. It's so unusual, he thought, with those stones on it. "He seems to like the down town area, and we've put out word that we're looking for him. It's a matter of time, I think, until we find him."

"Is he the one who's been watching Kat's house?"

Jace looked at Micah, then at Tracker. "Watching her house? We didn't know about that."

Micah and Nathaniel exchanged glances, then Micah continued, "At least twice the police have found evidence of someone watching Kat's house. The first was just after she moved in. The second time was the night we spent there when we came back from our honeymoon. They found a crumpled newspaper turned to our wedding announcement."

"That changes everything, Micah." Tracker walked away, and they could see her pacing outside Jace's door. She reappeared. "I don't need to warn you, Micah. This is escalating. Do everything you can to keep her safe and in your sight."

"That's what we're trying to do, but it's hard when she works at the college two days a week and I'm busy with the training in security. I know she's considering not teaching in the new semester."

Tracker nodded, her russet pony tail swinging in movement with her head. "That would likely be best, if it takes that long. Somehow, I don't think it will." With that cryptic remark, she walked away.

Later that week, Micah turned as Kat entered their kitchen. Matt, Luke and Murphy were there, handing each other cups of coffee. Kat walked into Micah's arms for his greeting, then turned to greet the other three men.

"I'm off to my office, guys. Enjoy your Bible study."

Micah stepped back to watch her walk down the hall, then reached for the fridge door. "Kat said she left something special for us tonight, and she was right." He pulled out a box from The Irish Charm, a local bakery, and opened it.

"Your wife spoils us, you know, Micah." Matt peeked into the box. "How did she know?"

"She listens and remembers. Her mind can be scary at times."

Settling down in the living room and picking up their Bibles, the four men settled into their study of God's truth. Time passed quickly, and the three men headed out, pondering the truths they had gleaned that night, strengthened from their time spent in God's Word and prayer with one another.

Micah stopped at the doorway and watched Kat at work. He finally walked over and took the pen from her hand. She leaned back and studied him, a slow smile crossing her face.

"Did they like their treats?"

Micah perched on the desk and nodded. "They did. They'll be telling the other guys how spoiled they were." He watched as her smile widened. "You didn't, did you?" At her nod, he shook her head. "You spoil all of us, you know that."

"You guys deserve it. Now, whose is the next wedding? I'm hearing rumours."

Micah stared at her. "The next wedding? What are you hearing?"

"You haven't heard?" When he shook his head, she laughed. "I'm hearing Matt and Sarah."

He thought about that, then nodded. "They were the first engaged of us guys. It makes sense."

Kat nodded as well. "It does. I think we started off the snowball of weddings, you know."

"I think we did. All through for the night?"

She looked at her desk, thought about it, and then nodded. "Just some tests that need to be marked, but I can do that tomorrow." She stood and stretched. "When do you guys head out again?"

Micah stared at her. "How do you do that?"

"Do what?"

"Read Abe's mind?"

She laughed. "I have no idea. I just get these feelings and know you're going to be heading out."

"He says Tuesday next week and back on Saturday morning. He's been asked to check out security on a new building."

"Sounds safe enough."

Micah watched her face. "But you don't think so?"

She shrugged. "I don't, but I have nothing to base that on."

"Just pray that God keeps us safe."

Chapter 14

Abe watched his men on the Thursday and listened to them. They were sniping at one another, and that was not them. He turned to look around and felt such a sense of evil it staggered him. He approached his team one by one and told them to head for the vehicles, they were leaving.

Once back at the hotel, Abe called a team meeting. He searched the faces of the men seated around the room and then nodded to himself. They were done here and would be on the road home that night.

"What's going on, Abe? What's happened this time?" Luke spoke for the men. "We never go after each other like this."

"I don't know, Luke, but it feels like we were set up somehow. When I pulled you out, I felt such a sense of evil I knew we couldn't stay." He turned as a knock came at the door.

Opening it, he found the head of security that had hired them.

"What's the meaning of this, Finlay? You can't pull out. You were hired to do a job." Adams' face was flushed with anger.

"No, we were hired to check out security. Your building is a joke. There is no security there." Abe stared at the man, then turned as Murphy called his name.

"Abe, that building just imploded. If you hadn't pulled us out, we'd have been buried."

Abe spun to stare at Adams, who was staring at Murphy in shock.

"That can't be right."

Joseph flicked on the television and there is full colour they watched the smoke and debris settling down.

Abe was furious. "You almost had my whole team killed, Adams. Are you responsible for this?"

He shook his head. "No, I'm not. You must have set the explosives."

Abe grabbed his arm and jerked him from the room, nodding for Murphy and Nathaniel to follow him. "Pack our stuff, guys. We'll meet at the plane. We're heading home."

Abe strode into the local police department, pushing Adams ahead of him, asking for the police chief.

After explaining who he was and what happened, the police chief stared at Adams.

"This isn't the first time he's tried something like this, but we've never been able to catch him. You've done us a real service, Abe."

"Do me a favour? Find out who hired him. The wife of one of my men has been targeted by someone after a computer program she wrote, and my gut feeling is that he's involved somehow."

"Computer program? Kat Evans?"

Abe stared at him, then nodded. "You've heard of it?"

The chief nodded. "We used it once a couple of years ago. It's not common knowledge who wrote it, but I happened to meet her just after we had an opportunity to test it. You say she's married now?"

"She is, to my team member Micah O'Connor. We're trying desperately to find out who's responsible for the text messages and death threats."

The chief stared into the distance, then looked back at Abe. "He's not going anywhere for a while, that's for sure. We'll see what we can dig up for you. He's not smart enough to have come up with this on his own, and to target you at this time, someone is behind it."

Micah settled into his seat in the plane and laid his head back. He was tired, no exhausted. The last three days had taken a toll on all of them, and he was glad he was headed home. It would be morning before they landed, but he hoped that Kat would be around.

Finally able to head for his home, Micah noted that Kat's car was in her parking spot and his steps quickened. Calling for her as he opened the door, he stopped, puzzled when he didn't see or hear her. Searching the house, he stopped in the kitchen. Her supper from last night sat there, partially eaten. He turned for the bedroom and saw her purse sitting on the dresser where she always left it. He spun in a circle, trying to think of where she could be.

He headed for Rebecca and Gideon's, then saw their cars were gone. Abe, watching Micah, headed for him.

"Micah! What's wrong?"

Micah turned as Abe approached, worry on his face. "I can't find Kat. Her car's here and her supper from last night is still on the table, not eaten."

Abe froze, then grabbing Micah's arm, headed for the business office. "Joseph's there. We'll have him run the security from last night." He pulled out his phone and dialed his sister's number. "Rebecca, have you seen Kat?"

"Just briefly late yesterday afternoon. She was planning on staying in, she said. Why?"

"She's not here. Micah can't find her in the house, and her car's still here."

He heard Rebecca gasp, then say something to someone.

"Gideon and I are on our way back."

Micah paced as he waited for Joseph to pull up the security video from yesterday. His heart in his mouth, he prayed that Kat had left with someone safe, but he didn't think so, not after what they had gone through. He had a sinking feeling they were lured away so someone could get to Kat.

"Here we go, Abe, from around 4 yesterday." Joseph looked past Abe at Micah as he turned and came close to watch the video.

"Fast forward for a bit, Joseph. I would say around 6?" Abe looked at Micah for confirmation.

He nodded. "She says she eats around 5:30 or so if she's on her own. We eat when we get to it when I'm home."

Then, as they watched, they saw a dark-clad, hooded man with his hand on Kat's arm leading her away from the compound, towards the gate. She hadn't struggled at first, then she started to. They watched as she broke free and ran back towards her home. Micah winced when she was tackled to the ground and her assailant knelt on her back. She struggled to get away, almost making it once, until her hands were roughly dragged behind her back and bound. She still struggled, at one point putting up enough of a fight the man's hood was knocked back and they were able to get a clear picture of his face.

"Freeze that, Joseph, and send it to the printer. I want to get it to Caleb." Abe turned to Micah, his heart breaking for his friend. "Do you recognize him?"

Micah shook his head. "Go on with the feed, Joseph. See what else is there."

They watched, helpless, as Kat was dragged from their security compound and through the gate, to disappear from sight. Micah sank back into a chair. His worse fears had come true. Kat had been abducted when he wasn't here to prevent it.

Caleb turned as he heard Frankie call his name. He didn't like the grim look on his face.

"Kat's been abducted from her home, sometime last evening."

"From Abe's?"

Frankie nodded. "She was the only one there and should have been safe with the security Abe has in place. Her abductor came right in through the front gate. Joseph managed to get a picture of him off the feed and is on his way in with it." He looked around. "I've sent a team out to Micah's but I'm not optimistic we'll get much."

Frankie looked past Abe as Joseph appeared at the front counter and headed towards him. Walking back with Frankie,

Joseph explained what they had seen in the security video.

Caleb stared at him for a minute, then pointed towards the conference room. "Find your team, Frankie, and get set up. I'll have everything we have pulled and sent there. You have a photo, Joseph?"

Joseph handed over the folder he had been holding. "I made extra copies for you. Nathaniel was heading for Tracker's with a copy."

Caleb nodded as he opened the folder, his hand stilling as he stared at the man's face. "I know this face." He tapped the photo. "I know him from about five years ago, but his name escapes me at the moment. It will come to me." He looked up at Joseph. "Do me a favour? Take a copy to Ben Johnson. He may remember him. If I recall, he had a run in with him about that time."

Joseph nodded, then stopped when Caleb called his name.

"What was that, Caleb?"

"How's Micah?"

Joseph stared at his friend, then shook his head. "Devastated is the word I would use. He's lost half of himself right now, Caleb, as I'm sure you understand."

Caleb nodded, then sighed. "Pray we find her quickly."

Frankie turned as Caleb entered the conference room, which had turned into a beehive of activity. "Joseph headed out?"

Caleb looked around, then spoke. "I sent him to see Ben. Ben had a run in with that fellow. I just wish I could remember his name."

"I started someone searching your arrests around that time, hoping we can find him."

"I don't recall arresting him, but there should be a report of some kind. He wasn't from here, but from Oak City if my memory's correct."

Chapter 15

Nathaniel stepped into the reception area at Tracker's and waited. Tracker, heading for the break room, stopped, stared at him and then came towards him.

"Nathaniel, what brings you here?" Her gray eyes studied him.

Nathaniel swallowed hard against the lump in his throat. "It's Kat."

Tracker took another look at him, then beckoned him to follow her. Pointing to the armchair at her desk, she sat on her desk.

"What about Kat?"

"She was abducted from her home last night. We were away, on a setup by someone who wanted us out of the way, so they could get to Kat."

Tracker nodded. "That's what I was afraid of." She nodded at the folder he held. "What's that?"

Nathaniel handed it over. "Joseph was able to pull a clear picture of the man. Kat put up quite a fight and almost got away."

Tracker opened the folder, and as she stared at the photo, her whole body stilled. Then, she was up and at her computer, fingers flying as she pulled up website after website, finally stopping.

"I have a name for you, Nathaniel, as well as a long list of aliases. Here, let me print it out for you." She turned from her printer, papers in hand, and studied him. "I have to warn you, though, this man is not a nice man. He's muscle for hire, as I would presume you have already figured out."

Nathaniel nodded as Jace appeared in Tracker's doorway.

"What's up, Tracker? Kat?"

She nodded and pointed to her screen. "Him."

"We've been after him for years now, almost since when we started up. Let's pray this time we catch him."

"Thanks. We appreciate this." Nathaniel stood, hesitating for a minute. Then he shook his head and walked away.

Jace stepped back to watch him. "Do you think they'll find her in time?"

Her eyes on her desk top, Tracker shrugged. "I pray they do, but that's not the record with this man. Everyone he has abducted has been found dead. We need to pray, Jace. I like Micah. I don't want to see that happen to him."

Jace agreed. He turned to walk back to his desk, then changed his mind and headed for his car. He would go talk with Frankie and see what he could do to help.

Abe watched as Micah paced the yard. Here we go again, Lord. Another lady in trouble, and we can't find her. Guide our search, Lord. Give my friend the strength he needs to get through this. He turned as he heard his name called. Ian and Murphy stood beside him, eyes on their friend.

"It's been six days, Abe. We can't get Micah to eat, barely get any fluid into him." Murphy's words caught at Abe.

Abe nodded. "I know. We can't force him." He looked towards the office. "Matt and Sarah are taking this hard. They want to put off their wedding next week."

Ian nodded. "Micah won't hear of it, though. He's told them to go ahead.

Somehow, he has a confidence that Kat will be found before then.”

Abe looked at Ian, then back at Micah. “He’s never said that to me.”

“It just popped out last night when we were praying. This is making his faith stronger, if anything.”

Kat turned blurry eyes towards her abductor. It had been a week since she had been abducted from her home. She had been negligent in locking her door that night, hoping that Micah would be home. The man had been upon her before she even knew he was in the house. She had been dragged out and towards the gate, finally recovering her wits enough to fight him. She had almost made it away from him, heading for safety, when he tackled her. She had the bruises, cuts and scrapes from that.

She was shoved down into a chair in front of a computer. Her mind foggy, she barely heard the command she had been hearing once a day for the last week. There was no way she would bring up her program for him to use. Lack of food and water was taking its toll on her, and her thought processes were dimming. She shook her head at the man, refusing to do what he asked. She heard his yells and curses, then his rough hands yanking her from the chair and thrusting her back into the room she had been held it. She stumbled and sank to the floor, her eyes closing as she drifted off, her last thought a prayer for Micah.

Day eight, she was once again dragged to the computer and shoved down in front of it. She nodded as she was once more asked for the program. Setting her fingers to the keyboard, she hesitated. Lord, what I'm about to do hurts so much. This program has brought out truth in so many cases, but it's not worth the risk to Micah's life. They'll go after him if I don't do something, Kat thought.

Head pounding, she started keying in her passwords. The man stood behind her, glee on his face as he held his phone and spoke into it, acknowledging that Kat was working her way into the program and would soon turn it over to them.

At the last password, Kat hesitated. She blinked to clear her eyes. This is it, Lord. I'll not likely live to see Micah again. Protect him and heal his sorrow, dear Lord. She typed the last lengthy password and the program was up. Her fingers not stilling on the keyboard, she continued to type, reaching her failsafe program that would destroy the program.

As the data began to disappear from the screen, the man behind her froze, then started screaming at her, curses and vile language filling the room. He stared in shock as the program disappeared and a screen came up saying that the program was not available.

He turned to her, hand flying across her face, knocking her to the floor. Dragging her to her feet, he shoved her back to the room she had been locked it, not caring that his violence sent her to the floor. He stared at her as his rage built. He had promised that he would get the program for his buyer and now it no longer existed. He walked heavily towards her, and stood over her. He finally walked away, leaving her a crumpled broken heap in the middle of the floor, his fists and feet leaving their mark on her.

Nathaniel looked up from the book he was trying to read as Abe stepped through the door at Micah's home.

"Where's Micah?"

Nathaniel nodded towards the bedroom. "I finally got him to go lie down." Nathaniel stopped, trying to control his emotions. "I checked on him a while ago. He's asleep, Kat's bathrobe in his arms. Abe, I haven't see him cry all this time. While he's sleeping, he's crying. The tears just don't seem to stop."

Abe's eyes slid shut. He knew that feeling, missing someone so much that the tears flowed when he slept.

"Can you get him up? Frankie called. He wants us at the hospital."

"They've found her?"

Abe nodded. "He said they had found where she was and were headed in to get her."

Nathaniel turned from where he had been heading and studied Abe's face. "What didn't he say?"

Abe shrugged. "I don't think they know anything yet."

Nathaniel stood watching his friend for a moment, then reached to shake Micah awake. "Wake up, buddy. Abe's here."

Micah blinked, then sat up. "Abe's here?"

Nathaniel nodded. "Come on, up you get and get yourself together."

Abe watched as Micah stumbled slightly from fatigue and lack of food as he entered the living room.

"Abe, have you news?" Micah was desperate to hear Kat had been found.

Abe nodded. "Frankie called. He wants us to head for the hospital. They've found where Kat is being held."

Micah's eyes slid shut. Thank you, Lord. Just let her be alive, please. He reached for his phone as it chimed and stared at the screen. "She did it. She really did it."

"Did what, Micah?" Abe and Nathaniel shared a puzzled look.

"She hit the fail-safe portion of her program. That destroyed it." He looked up, fear for his wife in his face. "That means they have no reason to keep her alive now."

Abe and Nathaniel exchanged a grim look. Would it be a rescue or recovery that Doug's team was going in on?

"Let's get you into town, Micah. Frankie was hopeful they'd be on their way to the hospital quickly."

Doug Foster, lieutenant on the first squad ETF, briefed his men, then turned to Caleb. "We're set, Caleb. Dave and Tom are ready to come in when we call?"

Caleb turned, searching for the paramedics Doug had named. "They are.

I've got a cruiser in place in front of them, and cruisers ready to block intersections where and when needed. Go. Find Kat and bring her out."

Doug's team hit the door of the decrepit building, entering and searching room by room. Finally, a locked door stood in their way. On a count of three, the door was down, and Doug and his second-in-command entered, searching for the culprit. Then, their eyes were drawn to the form on the floor. Heart in mouth, Doug crouched and reached to feel for a pulse. It was faint and seemed to be getting fainter under his fingers. He turned his head and sent word for Dave and Tom.

Caleb watched as Dave and Tom feverishly worked on Kat, trying to keep her alive long enough to reach the hospital.

"Caleb, we have an escort?" Dave finally looked up.

"It's all set, Dave. Go. I'm closing off intersections for you as well." Caleb reached to help carry the stretcher down the stairs and then outside. He nodded to the officers assigned to the escort. "Go, fellows. Get her there."

Frankie stood beside him. "Abe was bringing Micah in. I hope he's in time."

Caleb's heart was heavy. "I hope so, too, Frankie. Nathaniel got word to me that Kat hit the failsafe on her program and destroyed it."

Frankie nodded. "That's what set this off." He looked around. "We have a lot of work to do right here. I pray we find some evidence to track this guy down."

"I can guarantee he's not the one who instigated this. Somewhere out there, a buyer is very unhappy. We need to keep a guard on her at all times. I'll talk to Abe. Micah won't be safe either."

"No, he won't." Frankie turned as an officer approached him.

"Frankie, we found the computer she used. We're heading to the lab with it, but I'm not sure if we'll find anything on it. It looks like a brand new one."

Caleb nodded. "That would be par for the course. See if we can track who bought it."

Micah was out of Abe's truck and at the back door of the ambulance as the stretcher holding Kat was offloaded. He reached to touch her, keeping pace as Dave and Tom pushed the stretcher into an exam room. Dave's eyes watched as Micah stood as close as he could while they were giving their report. He knew nothing would get Micah from that room.

Frenzied activity that seemed mindless and useless filled the room. Micah's eyes stayed on his wife despite this. Finally, a nurse approached him.

"You need to leave."

Micah shook his head. "No. I'm not leaving."

"Yes, you need to leave."

Micah shrugged off her hand and moved closer to Kat.

Despite her constant demands he leave, Micah ignored her. Finally, she rang for security, even though the nurses in the room told her to leave Micah alone. She strode for the door, opening to find men standing in her way. She pushed through and turned to glare at Joseph, Murphy and Ian standing guard at the door, a police officer bedside them. Spying the two security men, she pointed at the room she had just left.

"Get that man out of there. He's not to be in there."

Just staring at her, the men refused to move and follow her instructions. Anger driving her, she once again ordered them to remove Micah.

A hand found her arm and dragged her away from the door, the security men following. Dr. John Thompson stood there, anger in his face.

"That is enough, Debbie. These men will escort you to the nursing supervisor. You will remain there until I make my report. You won't be working in my Emergency Department anymore." He held up a finger as she went to speak. "Not another word. I'll give you slack because you likely don't know the situation, but if you know it and have continued to ignore it, acting like you have, I'll see that you won't work in a hospital in the area ever again." He nodded to the security men.

The older of the men stopped him as he went to walk away. "We wouldn't have removed him, Dr. Thompson. We know the story."

"Thank you." John nodded at Abe's men as he pushed through the door into the room. "What do we have, Susan? Talk to me."

Shooting a quick look at Micah, John commenced his own examination, calling for imaging studies, bloodwork, and then for the surgeon on call to be paged.

Dr. Amos Johns pushed the door open to the room as John was studying the imaging results. He stood beside him, their quiet conversation filling the room. Dr. Johns stepped away from the computer monitor holding the images and examined Kat's left side, pointing to an area.

"I agree, John. We need to go up to the operating room now. I'm headed up, but first, her next of kin?"

John nodded at Micah. "That's her husband. They've only been married a few weeks."

Dr. Johns shot him a look, then approached Micah, who reluctantly dragged his eyes from Kat. "Micah, we're heading into surgery with Kat. Whoever did this…" Dr. Johns' voice failed him. "What I'm trying to say is that there is damage on her left side. We have a piece of rib really close to the cardiac sac and we need to fix that. We've got her stabilized enough to attempt it."

"Attempt it?" Micah's weary eyes searched the surgeon's face. "You're not sure you'll be successful?"

Dr. Johns shook his head. "No, I'm not, Micah. I know you and your friends have great faith. She's the pastor's cousin, I understand? Then he'll have the prayer chain going." He turned and watched as Kat was wheeled from the room. "I'm heading in there now. It'll be a few hours, I suspect. I'll come find you in the surgical waiting room. I'll make sure you get regular updates."

Micah nodded, his eyes watchful. Abe entered the room, and stopped, eyeing his friend.

"Micah?"

Micah turned, not bothering to hide the tears.

"Micah? What's going on? We saw them taking Kat up to surgery, John said."

Micah nodded, then pushed away from the wall he had been leaning on, staggering as he did so. Abe caught him as he fell, his shouts bringing John back to the room. A call for a stretcher and Micah was soon being examined. His eyes drifted shut and he slept, tormented by thoughts of life without Kat.

"What happened, Abe?" John's eyes sought his as he examined Micah.

"Micah hasn't eaten at all, or even drank much liquid since he found Kat missing." Abe watched his friend's face, seeing the devastation there.

"About what I expected. Look, I'll run blood work and an IV. That will help." He looked around at the nurse and gave quiet orders. "I'll leave him here for now, but in about two hours, I'll have him taken up to the surgical waiting room. I'll get word to Dr. Johns what's going on."

Abe nodded. "I heard about that nurse. Don't let her near him."

John snorted. "She's gone from the hospital. She's on administrative leave, not returning here by our choice. She won't work in a hospital in the area now at all."

Abe shook Micah's shoulder a couple of hours later. Micah roused, his eyes blurring as he stared around him, finally focusing on Abe.

"Abe, what happened?"

"You fainted, Micah. John's had a look at you. Right now, we want to move you up to the surgical waiting room. The nurse was out about thirty minutes ago and told Greg it was going as well as it could and that it would be a few more hours."

Micah's eyes slid shut. "She's still alive, then?" He opened his eyes to see Abe's nod. He went to sit up and the room spun around him.

Abe's eyes went to Matt standing at Micah's head. "Careful there, buddy. We've a wheelchair for you. John won't let you walk."

Chapter 16

Micah settled into a chair in the waiting room, IV still in his arm. He studied it, watching the fluid drip drop by drop down the line. He laid his head back, a headache developing behind his eyes. He knew his team members and their ladies were there, and that Gideon and Rebecca were too. He roused at a hand on his arm and looked up to see Greg standing there.

"Greg." His voice was hoarse.

"Micah. How are you?" At Micah's shrug, he nodded. "About what I thought." Greg sank into a chair beside him. "Did Abe tell you the nurse was out a while ago looking for you?"

"He did. Thanks for taking the information, Greg. No further word?"

Greg shook his head. "I've spoken with my uncle. They're preparing to head this way in the next few hours. I understand your brothers are coming tonight."

Micah nodded. "Likely, but they shouldn't. Mom's facing heart surgery. They should be there."

"She's sending them, Micah, to be with you when she can't." Micah's eyes turned to watch him. "Listen, Micah. I know Kat is your world. God has her in His hand."

Micah sighed. "I know, Greg. I know that, but it's hard to accept what He may be asking of me." He looked up as a nurse in scrubs approached him.

"Mr. O'Connor?" At his nod, she dropped into the chair beside him. "Don't look so worried. Your wife is in good hands. Dr. Johns asked me to come find you. He thinks about another thirty minutes and Kat will be moved to recovery. She's done well. He'll give you a full report, but it will be a while after she's in recovery that he'll come find you. He wants to stay with her for now to ensure everything's all right."

"Thank you, nurse." Micah watched as she walked away, then his eyes caught movement from the room. His team members had stood when the nurse entered the room and their eyes were on him. He beckoned to Abe.

"Abe, let them know she's coming through all right by what the nurse said. She'll be in recovery soon."

Abe's eyes slid shut as he said a prayer of thanks. He nodded, then turned to find his team members waiting for him. Micah could see the relief in their bearing at Abe's words.

Micah's eyes slid shut as he dozed. He jerked awake at a hand on his arm and looked up to see Dr. Johns standing in front on him. The doctor sank into a chair beside him and waited for a minute to gather his thoughts.

"Doctor?" Micah's voice was hesitant.

"She's being moved to an ICU room and then you can go see your lady, Micah. It was touch and go for most of the surgery. A rib piece ended up within a short distance of the heart sac. That would have killed her before she got here, if it had moved any further. God was looking after your lady." He stared ahead as he once more gathered his thoughts. "She's been beaten, badly I must say. Lots of bruises, some cuts. Her ribs on the left side took the brunt of the beating. We've repaired them, but she'll be laid up for quite a while. We're keeping her in a drug-induced coma for now to allow for healing and pain control." He stood, looking down at

Micah. "I'll find you when we get her settled."

Micah stood and walked away from the waiting room. He needed some space. Frankie stood watching him, then followed. At the footsteps behind him, Micah turned, stopping as he saw Frankie.

"Frankie, what's the word on the investigation?"

Frankie shook his head. "Not where we want it, Micah. We have some evidence but not enough to figure out who it is. How's Kat?"

"She's come through the surgery and will soon be in an ICU room. I just wish I had been home and prevented this."

Frankie nodded. "I know, Micah. Jace has come up with a name for us, based on the picture Joseph pulled. We're circulating it in the down town area."

Micah stopped walking, his thoughts going to the picture. "There's something odd about that, Frankie. How did he get through our security? Joseph can't find any way that he did. An alarm should have alerted us, even though we were away from home."

"Joseph's looking into that. He says it looks as if the circuit was blocked for the length of time the man was on the property. How, he's not yet certain."

"That makes sense. So, where do we go from here, Frankie?"

"We're working it through, Micah. The team seized a computer Kat had to work on. We've found some evidence I can't discuss, but we're hoping someone comes through who saw the man in the area. Once we find him, we'll work to find the man responsible."

"What about that man Abe had the run in with when we were away?"

Frankie pulled out his phone as it vibrated. Wilson! "Wilson, talk to me. What do you have?"

"Not what you want to hear." Jake Wilson's voice was hard and furious. "We found the man, but he's dead. Shot execution style."

"Well, that's that then. Anyone see anything?"

"We're working that. But he had a paper in his pocket. Micah's now a target for sure as is Kat. Whoever this guy was working for, he's not happy."

Frankie slowly pocketed his phone, his thoughts racing. This just put a whole new outlook on the case. He looked up to find Micah's eyes on him.

"They found him, didn't they, Frankie? And let me guess, he's dead." Micah's words spit out in a furious, angry manner. Frankie stared at him. This was so not Micah.

He nodded. "They did. Wilson also said they found evidence naming you as a target now, Micah. So, let's go find Abe and see what he has to say."

Abe looked up as Frankie and Micah headed his way, knowing that it wasn't good.

"Frankie, what's wrong? I can tell something is by the look on your face." Abe stood from where he had been sitting and moved towards them.

Frankie was frustrated. "The man who kidnapped Kat? He's dead. But he had information on him making both Kat and Micah targets now. I hear she destroyed her program. That will bring out the anger even more."

Abe nodded, eyes staring into the distance. "That means we'll need to up the security on both Kat and Micah." He turned to Micah. "I know you won't be leaving here for now."

Micah held up his hand. "Stop right there, Abe. You can't pull the team just to provide security for me. Matt and Sarah's wedding is next week, and I won't have their celebrations leading up to it disturbed. So find a new solution." He stared at his friend. "We've tried this at least six times before and it's never worked out the way we wanted it to."

Abe nodded. "It hasn't. I'm bringing in a friend to help. The team Paul's with. They're coming in to provide security for you two, as well as our guys when we can."

Micah nodded, then looked past him at the surgeon heading his way. Without a word, he brushed past him to go meet him. A few words and Micah followed him back down the hall.

Abe stared after him. "This is a whole new ballgame for us, Frankie. Usually it's an engaged couple that we are trying to protect."

Frankie nodded. "It usually is. It might make it easier, keeping them together, but with Kat in the ICU, that changes it. Let me see what I can work out as well. Our people want this guy as much as you do. They don't like feeling they've been set up."

Micah stood at Kat's bedside, eyes on his wife, then raising to study the equipment beeping and humming around her, keeping her alive. He had been warned by Dr. Johns. She had survived the beating, the surgery, but she still had a long way to go. Even now, he had said, she might not make it.

Micah pulled his chair close and sank down, his heart crying out to God for healing for Kat, then for God's will to be done. Only God knew if she would survive. He reached for her hand and clasped it in his. It felt cold and lifeless.

Greg stopped in the doorway, heart breaking his friend. He turned and walked away, his doubts surfacing. How could he minister to Micah when he wasn't so unsure himself?

Chapter 17

Caleb scrubbed his hands down his face, weary to the bone. It hadn't been good news to hear the abductor was dead, and they had no lead on who had hired him. His detectives, he knew, were working frantically to find the man, but he had covered his tracks well. Jace had come up with a name, but the man had too many aliases for them to be searched through. They needed a break in the case, and he somehow didn't think one would come.

Eddie stood for a moment studying Caleb before he knocked at his door and entered. He sank into one of the chairs in front of Caleb's desk and slid his eyes closed. He too was weary and fatigued.

"What do you have, Eddie?" Caleb's quiet question reached him.

"The team is still going through his room at the motel. They tell me they've found some information, including a name they're trying to trace back. I spoke with the chief of the town where Abe had his trouble. The man was bailed out and then disappeared. The chief thought he was heading this way. If he's our man and was arrested and then released, I'm not sure how Abe and his team will handle it."

Caleb shook his head. "I don't even want to go there." He leaned back. "What else do we have?"

"The computer was bought with cash, so there's nothing there. It's clean, other than what Kat had brought up on it." Eddie was frustrated. "I just don't have anything I can work with, Caleb. If God was to give Hannah a name, I'd take it."

"About now, so would I. She hasn't come up with a name in a while, though."

"No, she hasn't. God has been silent that way with her."

Eddie stood, then turned back to Caleb. "Have you heard how Kat is?"

"She came through surgery and is in ICU. Abe's bringing in Don's team to help with security. His men have worked with them before."

Eddie shook his head. "I hate this, Caleb, even though I know God's in control.

It's like there's nothing we can do, nowhere we can turn to."

Caleb watched his friend. "Go talk with Ben. He may have an insight we don't. He has so many contacts we don't and never will have."

Eddie nodded. "That's where I'm off to."

Abe stood watching Micah, seeing the fear and anger in his friend. Lord, he prayed, we need resolution of this and I can't see it happening. Lead Caleb and his men to find this man, whoever it is. Knowing what Kat did will make him angry enough to come after her again, and if he can't get to her, he'll go after Micah. He turned as he heard his name called. He knew his team members had scattered to spend time with their fiancées and family.

"Don. Thanks for coming so quickly." Abe reached to shake his hand.

"You'd do it for me, Abe, if I asked. How is she?"

Abe nodded towards the waiting room. "Let's go sit. Kat's come through the surgery, but she's not out of the woods, not by a long shot. Micah's not leaving her side."

Don Woods nodded. "I hear you. Now, what can we do to help? All five of my guys are with me. Paul's hurting the most of us, having worked with your guys."

"I have a team in for training next week for four days. I need all my guys there at some point over the week. Matt's wedding is on Saturday. Micah is adamant that Matt not be involved in any security for him over the next few days."

Don looked down the hall towards the room Kat lay in, then back at Abe. "Walk me through what you want and need, and we'll make it happen. Two of us at a time for eight hours will work. I'm assuming your police chief is providing people as well?"

Abe nodded. "Caleb is. I think you two have met sometime in the past. Frankie Brennan and Eddie Brown are the lead investigators, so they'll be in and around."

"Eddie, I know quite well, actually. Frankie, I've met in passing. We'll work it out with them. Now, as to physicians, nurses, and other staff, we'll need to restrict those."

Abe agreed. "Dr. Amos Johns is her surgeon. I've made arrangements for only two nurses to be with her, twelve-hour shifts for each, for the next week or so. Dr. Johns can't say how long she'll be here." Abe's attention was caught by a man loitering in the hallway near the elevator. He brought out his phone and snapped a picture. "There's someone I don't think should be here. Do you want to go and talk with him?"

Don took a look at the man. "He looks familiar. Sure, I'll go see what he wants. The only way off is the elevators?"

Abe nodded. "Unless you have a pass to open the stairway doors."

As Don approached the man, he turned and slid into a closing elevator, disappearing from view. Abe walked over to Don.

"I would say he wasn't here to visit anyone."

Don agreed. "He was gone before I could get to him. You got his picture? Send it on to me and I'll circulate it with my guys."

"I'll do that. I'm also sending it to Jace at Tracker's and to Frankie. Maybe they can track down who it was." Abe stopped speaking. "He looked a little like the fellow I had a run in with last week, when we were doing security checks on a building. I pulled my guys just before the building imploded. He was arrested, but I'm told he made bail and disappeared."

"Now, that sounds a little suspicious, don't you think?" Don looked around. "I'm going to go find my guys and get us set to start your security." When Abe went to speak about cost, Don stared at him, then spoke, "There's no charge, Abe. It's what we do for friends. You've been there for me in the past." He turned and walked away.

Murphy spoke from behind Abe. "Is Don on board, Abe?"

Abe spun, not having heard Murphy approach. "He is. His team will be working in twos, on eight-hour shifts, for now. How are the guys?"

Murphy shrugged. "They're hurting, Abe, in a way I haven't seen before. With us all being engaged and looking into the near future for our weddings, we can put ourselves in Micah and Kat's spots, and we don't like what we're feeling."

Abe shook his head. "No, I don't think you would. Are you staying for now?"

"I thought I would. Adriel wants me to." He looked at his long-time friend. "What's going on, Abe? Whatever it is, it's more than just this."

Abe stared at Murphy, knowing that at some point he would have to talk to his friend. "Whatever it is, it's complicated, Murphy, and so deeply buried, I'm not even sure where to begin. It happened years ago."

"At the beginning is usually a good spot. I won't push you tonight, Abe, but know I'm here if you want to talk." Murphy hesitated. "I know this isn't a good time, but Adriel and I have been talking."

Abe smiled. "When's the wedding?"

Murphy shook his head. "A mind reader now, are we? We're thinking in about three weeks. We've decided we don't want to wait any longer."

"I figured Micah and Kat getting married would spur the rest of you on. I'll work you out of the rotation for the following week, Murphy."

Abe walked away at that point, headed for the elevators and home. Murphy watched him leave, then turned to the ICU room where he knew he'd find Micah.

Chapter 18

The man stood watching the ICU room Kat lay in. He looked around. She had too much security around her for him to get to her today. He could wait. She owed him. She owed him for leaving him destitute while she made money on that program. And then to destroy the program when he almost had it in his hands, that went beyond what he could accept. He turned for the elevator, reaching to push the button, and tossing his empty water bottle into the garbage.

Don watched as the man left, then approached a nurse, asking for a latex glove. He retrieved the water bottle and went searching for a paper bag. It just might be what cracked this case open. He pulled out his phone, ready to call one of the detectives, when Frankie walked off the elevator towards him. A few quick words, and Don handed Frankie the bag.

Frankie's eyebrows rose as he realized what Don was handing him. Was this it, Lord, he asked?

"Check this out, will you? The man who ditched it was watching Kat's room."

Frankie shot him a quick look, then looked back at the elevators. "I'll have someone pull the security tape. Maybe we'll find something there."

"I hope you do. My team can't stay for long, but I don't want to abandon Abe."

Frankie studied the man standing in front of him. "He won't think that, Don. He appreciates your team stepping up for now." Frankie looked down the hallway. "For now, we have her under police guard, but I'm not sure how long Caleb can let that go."

"It's always a difficult decision, knowing when to pull security." Don turned back to the elevators. "Check with my guys if you need anything."

Frankie walked quietly up to Micah, who turned as he approached. Frankie studied the face of his friend. Lord, we need Kat to wake up and we need to end this now.

"How is she, Micah?"

Micah shrugged. "They're talking about pulling the ventilator in a day or so and weaning back on the drugs she's on, hoping she'll wake up." Micah stared across the room. "Any word, yet, Frankie?"

Frankie shook his head. "Not yet, but we're working hard." He held up the bag Don had handed him. "Don found someone watching her room and confiscated a water bottle. I'm pulling security tapes to see what we can find."

Micah stared at him. "He was here, on this floor?"

Frankie shook his head. "We don't know that for sure, Micah. Let us work this through." Frankie looked down at his phone as it ran. "That's Jace."

He walked away to take his call, spinning to stare at Micah as he talked. Then he headed for the elevators. Jace had come through with a name, finally, to go with the picture Abe had forwarded on. Maybe, just maybe, the case would break.

Micah watched as Frankie left, then turned back to Kat. She was starting to move, and he could see the pain flickering across her face. Please, dear Lord, heal her. He reached for her hand as he sat. The nurses had gotten used to him being there, working around him.

Not one would ask him to leave, knowing what they had gone through.

Saturday, Micah sat between Gideon and Abe as he watched his team mate and friend, Matt, and his lady, Sarah. They make a great couple, he thought. Bless their marriage, please, dear Lord. Keep them both safe.

Micah stood in front of Sarah, a smile on his face for the first time in days he felt.

"Welcome to the family, Sarah," was his comment as he bent to drop a kiss on her cheek.

Sarah's head tilted as she watched his face and then nodded. "Thank you, Micah. You're in our prayers, dear friend."

Micah nodded, then moved to shake Matt's hand. Matt studied his friend, then pulled him into a hug.

"How's Kat today?" His question was quiet.

"She's rousing, Matt. Dr. Johns thinks that she'll be awake in the next day or so."

Matt nodded, knowing that he wasn't sure he would have the faith to go through what Micah and Kat were going through. He watched as his friend walked away, Sarah's hand tight on his.

Micah stood once again by his wife's bedside, wondering how the investigation was going. Don's team had had to head back home, and he was worried about Kat's safety. He knew Caleb would do his best, but his hands were tied as well. His team would be there, but they had people coming in for training, and he knew he had to be there at some point as well.

Kat stirred, her eyes flickering open and closed. Where was she? She couldn't remember why she hurt. Her eyes finally opened, and she blinked to clear them, staring around at the room she was in, taking in the equipment surrounding her. She reached for the mask on her face, desperate to remove it, and a hand stopped her. She turned, a frown on her face as she studied the man bent over her bed. Who was he, she thought?

Then, her mind cleared. Micah! He was safe.

"Micah!" Her voice was barely audible.

"Kat! Oh, sweetheart, you're awake. No, you need to leave the mask on." He laid his hand on her face, and she watched as tears glistened in his eyes. "You've come back."

She nodded, puzzled as to his words and as to why she hurt so much. Unable to keep her eyes open any longer, she slept.

Micah turned as Dr. Johns entered the room. "She was just awake, Amos."

Dr. Johns looked surprised, then hastened to her bedside. "She was? That's good news, Micah, very good news. I wasn't expecting that for a few more days." He bent over her, assessing her. When he straightened up, he watched as Micah stared as his wife's face. "By tomorrow, I'll have her in a private room, Micah. She's not needing ICU care now."

"That's good news, Amos. Thank you."

Frankie turned as he heard his name called. Jace was running towards him.

"Frankie, wait up. I have something else for you on that name." Jace stopped for a moment to catch his breath. "There's something odd about this. We ran facial recognition on that picture Abe sent us. It comes up as someone else as well."

Frankie stared at him. "What do you mean?"

"I mean that this fellow you're looking for has a family member with close facial features, as in a brother or even a twin."

"A twin or a brother?" Frankie thought about that. "Okay, so do we have a name for him?"

Jace nodded. "Tracker found him. You're not going to like who it is." He handed over the slip of paper with the name on it.

Frankie's eyes slid shut. "No, you're right. I don't like this. I just wish Kat was well enough to talk to."

"We'll keep you updated on anything we come across. Hope it helps."

Chapter 19

Micah gently set Kat down on the couch in their home. She was still hurting but was adamant that she would not lie down.

"Thank you, sweetheart." She cradled her side for a minute, then reached for Micah's hand, pulling him down beside her. "No one is saying anything, Micah. Talk to me. Tell me what's happening with the investigation."

Watching her face, Micah nodded. She did need to know what was going on.

"They're working on it, KitKat. Frankie said he'd be out later today to talk with you about some new developments."

"New developments? How far has that brought the investigation?" She tilted her head to study him.

Micah shrugged. "I'm not sure. Frankie hasn't said."

"You did say the abductor is dead?"

Micah wrapped her carefully in his arms. "He is. You don't have to worry about him."

Kat sat and thought about what she had gone through. "Micah, is that picture I showed you still around?" Something was puzzling her about it.

"I think it is." He rose and headed for the office, bringing it back with him. Once seated again, he handed it to her.

She studied it. Then her hand was to her mouth. "I know why he looks familiar. He looks like Bob."

"Bob? As in the instructor Bob?"

She nodded and looked up at him. "Yes, him. I need to access my computer."

"No, not right now. Frankie has that picture and a name that he was given and is working on."

She stared at him. "He has that, and no one bothered to tell me?"

"Draw in the claws, KitKat. You've been too sick to think about this kind of stuff."

"Still, I should have been told. I could have gone back to work with him and disappeared totally."

Micah rested his chin on her head as he thought that through. You've protected her so far, Lord. Please, please continue to do so.

"We don't know for sure how deep he's involved, if he even is."

"It would make sense that he is, or else he's dropped a word somewhere about the program that someone overheard." She sighed. "I'll have to wind down the trust now, Micah, and wrap it up."

He nodded. "I know. We'll work it through as we can." He looked up at a tap at the door, and then the door opened to reveal Rebecca.

"Hi! Is it okay to come in?"

Kat looked around Micah at Rebecca and smiled. "Rebecca. Please come in. It's nice to see you. Come, sit. Tell me what adventures in photography you've been up to."

Rebecca handed over an album to Kat. "This. I've had it ready for a few days. It's your wedding pictures."

Kat's face lit up with excitement as she took the book. Micah took one look as her and headed for the kitchen to make coffee. He knew it would be a while before Rebecca left.

Kat paged slowly through the photos, a smile growing on her face. She looked up at Rebecca, who was sitting uneasily in the chair near her.

"Rebecca, these are beautiful. God has given you such a talent." She reached out to hug her friend, wincing as the incision on her side pulled.

"Oh, Kat. Thank you. How are you feeling now?"

"Frustrated. Caged. Useless. How does that sum it up for you?" Kat had a spark of mischief in her eyes. "And I have someone who won't stop hovering over me." She knew Micah was standing behind her.

Rebecca started laughing at that, catching the answering gleam of mischief on Micah's face. "He's standing behind you, you know. You just might not get that cup of coffee he has for you."

"Oh, I'll get it all right. I'll just play the patient card." She winked at Rebecca as Micah laughed, then handed her the cup, then handed the second cup to Rebecca.

"Here you go, Rebecca. Can you stay for a while?" Micah needed to head for the business office to see what work awaited him, but he didn't want to leave Kat on her own.

Rebecca waved him away. "I can. That's why I'm here. Rachel's on her way as well."

"Oh, that's lovely. Some girl time. I need that." Kat's eyes went back to the photos. "Can I get some copies enlarged of these, Rebecca? I'd love one of the two of us standing hand in hand looking at each other."

Rebecca nodded. "There's another one I would like to enlarge as well. The one where you're standing with your back to him, he's wrapped you in his arms, and you're looking at each other. The stained-glass effect on you both is just beautiful."

Kat stopped at that photo. "You're right. That's the one, for sure." She looked up at a tap at the door, and Rachel, Gideon's sister, peeked in.

"Rachel, come in. How's Timothy?" Kat was getting to know the ladies in their group. Rachel was married to Ben's son, Timothy.

"He's well, thank you. But, how are you?"

"We're not discussing that today." The two other women laughed at the look on her face.

Abe stood in the office door, staring at Micah hard at work, then back through the door at Micah's home.

"Micah, didn't Kat come home today?"

Micah turned in his chair as he heard Abe speak. "She did. Rebecca's with her and I heard Rachel was heading there as well."

"How is she?"

Micah started to laugh. "She's getting feisty and wanting to work." He stopped and watched as Abe dropped into his own chair. "Where do we stand work wise, Abe?"

"Actually, fairly well. We have a team coming in next week, and then we're off for a day the following week." Abe knew Micah had concerns about being away. "Gideon's agreed to be around that day, so you can rest easy on that."

Micah nodded, then paused as he went to speak. "Kat had an interesting comment today. She asked for that photo, the one from her first seminar. She commented that one of the men looked like Bob Thomas."

"Bob? Is she thinking he's involved?"

Micah stared at the door, then glanced back at Abe. "She is, and that has her worried. Frankie said he'd be out sometime this afternoon. I hope he has good news for us."

Frankie tapped at Micah's door, staring around as he waited. He could feel the evil drawing near but couldn't figure out where it was coming from. He turned back to the door as he heard it open.

Kat stood, watching Frankie for a moment, then stepped back to let him in.

"Can I get you anything, Frankie?"

He shook his head, studying Kat's face. He could see fading bruises and healing cuts on her face. "How are you feeling, Kat?"

"Getting there, Frankie. I'm sore, tired, frustrated. Take your pick or add to it, if you like."

Frankie nodded, then pointed at the couch. "You should be sitting down, you know."

She sighed. "I know, but I'm so tired of staying still. Rebecca and Rachel just left, so I hadn't had a chance to sit back down." She looked at him as he took a seat. "Do I need to call Micah back over?"

Frankie shrugged. "It's up to you. He basically knows some of what I'm going to tell you."

"All right, then. I'm sure he'll be here soon, anyway. Rebecca was headed that way to let him know I would be on my own. Go ahead with what you have to say."

Frankie studied her face once more. "Okay, so this is where we're at. Not where we want to be, but it's been a long, hard process so far.

"Jace has put a name to your photo. It's Fred Thomas."

"Bob's brother?" Kat wasn't surprised.

"I think they're related somehow. We feel he hired your abductor, then had him killed when he failed to follow through with the program."

Kat sat in silence, then spoke, "Bob never knew about the program I developed. I had him as an instructor, but no one at the college knew about it either." She raised her eyes to Frankie. "So, how did he hear about it?"

"That's something we'll have to ask him when we find him. We haven't been able to talk to Bob, he's still in critical care with his heart. It is uncertain if we'll ever be able to."

Kat nodded, then paused, her face whitening. "That's where I've heard that phrase about the daisies and the forget-me-nots. Bob's wife was always quoting it." Her hands covered her mouth as she took in the ramifications of what she had remember. "Frankie, he has to have been involved, or else the flowers are being used to throw you off from the real person."

Micah stood watching his wife. Then his eyes went to Frankie. "Frankie, how far along in the investigation have you got?"

Frankie turned to look at him. "I was just getting to that with your wife, Micah. Sit. It may take a while."

Micah's arm slid around Kat as he pulled her close to him. "I heard you say something about the flowers, KitKat."

She turned to look at him. "Bob's wife was always quoting that. Does that mean he's involved, or is she?"

Frankie's hand froze as he was making notes, and he looked up at her. "Now, that's a possibility I hadn't thought of. We'll look into her background as well. What else have you remembered, Kat?"

She shook her head. "Not a lot, Frankie. My mind's been so foggy. I don't know if I gave a very coherent statement to you. I can remember looking up and that man was standing in the doorway. I tried to get away. For seven days, I refused to bring up the program. For seven days, I had no food, no water, nothing. You know what I did on the eighth day.

"I can remember hearing him talk to someone outside the door of the room." She stopped, a frown on her face as she struggled to remember. Her eyes shot up to Frankie. "It was a woman's voice one day, then a man's voice another day. I didn't recognise the man's but remembering that about the flowers, I wonder if it was Bob's wife. There has always been something about her I just can't put my finger on."

Frankie nodded. "We'll look into her. Now, your family tree program and crime. Can it be used in this case?"

"Not really. We would need to know more of their family history, parents, deceased siblings, that kind of thing. If you can find that for me, I'll run it."

"Eddie's talked to Ben, Micah. Ben's going to his old sources to see what he can find out for us."

"That's good. He had a lot." Micah tilted his head to look at Kat. "If there's nothing else today, Frankie, I think Kat needs to go lie down."

"Not that's important. The team's still running the evidence they found." Frankie stood, watching the couple in front of him. "I don't need to tell you to be careful until we catch whoever it is. I don't want to see Kat back in the hospital or you either, Micah."

Kat leaned back on Micah after Frankie had left. "So, we're really not that far ahead, are we?"

Micah shook his head. "Not really, I would say. And don't you try and solve it on your own, Kat. I know you're itching to get involved, but you need to heal. I came too close to losing you two weeks ago."

She nodded, then yawned. "Only two weeks? It seems so much longer. Micah, I think I'm ready to go lay down."

Micah stood and watched at Kat stared into her dresser drawer. "What's wrong, Kat?"

"I need to change, Micah, but I'm not sure what will be loose enough, so it doesn't pull on the incision." She looked up, tears near the surface. "Does everything have to be so hard right now?"

He reached into another drawer. "Try one of my T-shirts for now."

He watched as her eyes closed in relief, then tucked her into bed. She was asleep before he had finished. He stood for a few minutes, then turned to go to her office. He sat at her computer, then began pulling up secure websites, tracking down names and faces. He was determined that he would do everything he could to find the culprits.

Chapter 20

Nathaniel tapped at Micah's door and entered when Micah answered it.

"You've found something, Micah?"

Micah nodded. "Come this way. Frankie was here today and mentioned that they were looking at Bob Thomas as a suspect. Kat remembered Bob's wife quoting that combination of words about the flowers. I've done some research, and I need another pair of eyes to go over it."

"Lead me to it, Micah. I'd like to see this solved as well."

Micah handed Nathaniel the material he had printed and pointed at one of the arm chairs in the office. "Sit. I'm going to check on Kat, and then I'll be back with coffee."

Nathaniel read through the material, and then sat back to think it through. He absentmindedly took the cup Micah handed him. Finally, he looked up at Micah, who had his eyes on him.

"First things first, Micah. We need to make this a matter of urgent, diligent prayer that God will open up the avenues of the investigation and the truth will come through. Secondly, I think you need to get this to Jace and see what he can come up with."

Micah nodded. "I agree. Care to take a road trip across town tomorrow? You're not on the schedule, nor am I."

Nathaniel nodded. "That I can do."

The next morning found the two men sitting across from Jace once again. Micah handed over the material he had printed.

Jace took it, his eyes on Micah, then dropping to the material. "You've found a lot, Micah. Any particular reason you started researching these names?"

Micah nodded. "Kat mentioned that Bob's wife quoted something about the flowers that was in that package."

Jace nodded, then turned to his computer. After searching, he suddenly pulled out his phone.

"I need to talk with Tracker. She'll have insight into this woman, I think." He waited for Tracker to answer, his phone on speaker.

"This had better be good, Jace. I'm on personal time here. If I had known it was you, I wouldn't have answered." Tracker's voice was tense.

"Tracker, listen to me for a minute. I have Micah and Nathaniel here. They've brought in a new name, a Nancy Thomas."

"Just a minute, Jace. I'll be right back." Her voice faded, but they could faintly hear her. "There, that's what I want. Come on, beautiful. Just a little closer. Right there. Perfect. Just a little bit closer, okay?"

"Tracker?" Jace's voice was patient but relentless is trying to get her attention.

"I got it, Jace. I finally got it. Ten feet away from me if that far." They could hear the jubilation in her voice.

"The one you've been after for years? Wonderful. Now, can we get back on track, Tracker?"

"Bad pun there, Jace. So, what's the name? Nancy Thomas? Let me think for a minute." They could hear the sounds of her pacing. "Got it. Try Betty Allen or Grace Twinings. She's used both of those in the past. How does she fit in?"

"The instructor Kat has worked with, Bob Thomas? It's his wife."

Tracker was silent for a moment. "Then, look for her sister, Janet, and her brother, William, as well. Bob has a brother, George, as well as a sister, April. Some of them skirted pretty close to the line, if not crossing over. I've got to go. Let me know, Micah, if there's something else."

She was gone before Jace could say another word. He looked up to the surprised looks on the two men's faces.

"How does she do that, Jace?" Nathaniel was trying to work through how she came up with the names.

Jace shrugged. "She just does. She can't explain it, but she's always right on with the names and relationships."

Micah took the paper Jace offered him. "I'll get this to Frankie. Maybe, just maybe, we'll catch a break. I pray we do." He looked up at Jace. "Care to explain what that was about with Tracker?"

Jace sat back, starting to laugh. "She goes out to the mountains every once in a while, to, as she says, fly with the eagles. There's been a pair she's followed for a while now and has been trying to catch a photo of them. She finally succeeded today." He stopped speaking, lost in thought. "She told me once that if she ever got that picture, then she knew what had happened to her in the past would be resolved in a short while. She's never said what it was."

"She sounds like Abe. Something happened in his past and he won't or can't talk about it. Thanks, Jace." Nathaniel stood to leave. "I would love to see that picture someday."

"I'll let her know. Take care, guys."

Nathaniel looked at Micah as he drove away. "Do any of those names sound familiar to you?"

Micah shook his head. "Do me a favour? I want to drop this off to Frankie, But I want a copy to run by Kat. She may know them."

Frankie looked up as Micah appeared in his doorway. "Didn't I just see you yesterday?"

"You did. I just spoke with Jace and Tracker. Tracker came up with some names and aliases for Bob's wife and family members. Here's the list."

Frankie took it, his eyes on Micah. "How does she do that?"

Micah shrugged. "We asked Jace the same thing. The thing of it was, she wasn't even in the office. She was off on some mountain somewhere, Jace said."

Frankie sat back, startled at the thought of how Tracker's mind worked. "I wish she'd come work with us. We'd have every case solved in a day."

Micah laughed. "You just might. Let me know what you find. I'm going to run them by Kat as well."

Kat stirred as she felt Micah sit on the edge of the bed.

"Good morning, sweetheart. Ready to rise and shine?" Micah's voice was quiet as he watched for signs of pain and distress in her face.

She blinked, then nodded. "I think so. I don't remember even going to bed last night."

"No, I didn't think you would. Listen, Nathaniel and I have been to see Jace. Tracker came up with some names. Once you're up and had your breakfast, I'd like to run them by you. I have to be in the training building this afternoon, so I was hoping we could work through some of the information this morning."

Mid-morning, Kat rose from her computer and starting pacing. She had been through the material Micah had found, checked out the names Tracker had given him, and felt no further ahead in her quest for the truth.

"Micah, what are we missing? There has to be something." She looked around. "This is when I miss the chalkboard, where I can scrawl out all the information."

Micah looked up at her, then reached for the material. "Come on. We have a board in the office we can use. Maybe one of the other guys will have an idea of what we're missing."

She nodded, a thoughtful look on her face. "You know, I'm really not sure about Bob any more. Who knows what he's picked up over the last five years we've done the seminars."

"That's what I'm afraid of, Kat, that he's found something he shouldn't have and was using it or let it slip." Micah paused, looking at her. "Have you had any more of those text messages?"

She shrugged as she searched for her phone. "I can't find my phone. Have you seen it?"

Micah searched as well. "Here. It looks as if you left it in the kitchen when you were abducted."

Kat reached slowly for the phone, a thought crossing her mind. "You know, I was recording some thoughts for a new seminar that night. I can't remember if I stopped recording or not."

Micah's eyes flew to her face, then back to her phone, as he reached for it. "It's on here?"

She nodded. "Let me see if I can find it for you." She scrolled through, then stopped at an application. "Try this. It might have it on it."

Micah searched Kat's face, looking for any signs of distress. She was calm, as if she knew the end of her troubles was coming. He started the application and hear Kat's voice, then the sound of a man. He listened through until he heard the door slam, then stopped it.

"Kat, do you know who that was?"

She shook her head. "I didn't know him. Take that to Frankie. He can search through with his team." She looked at the clock. "On second thought, have Frankie come out here, if you can. You're due to go to the training building in a little while."

Micah nodded, frustrated that he held a clue in his hand, but had to set it aside for the moment. "I'll see if he can come out late this afternoon. I should be done by about 3:30."

"In the meantime, can you gather my material and we'll head for the office for me to use the board.?"

"You'll tell us what you want to write. You can't be stretching the muscles on that side yet."

She sighed, knowing he was right. "Micah, whose wedding is coming up? I can't remember what you told me."

"It's Murphy and Adriel. Then the next Friday night, it's Joseph and Leah. They're staying around until the Saturday night as Luke and Abi are getting married on the Saturday."

Kat grinned. "I think we started something there, sweetheart."

Micah dropped a kiss on her mouth. "I think we did. That will just leave Nathaniel and Elizabeth and Ian and Lydia. Nathaniel said they're planning in about two weeks, and Ian said two weeks later for them."

"What about Abe?"

Micah shrugged. "We have never seen Abe date anyone in all the time we've known him. He has just never shown interest in anyone."

"I think he has already given his heart to a lady, Micah. What happened there, I don't know. There's something in his eyes every once in a while that makes me think that."

Micah hugged his wife, before heading for the door, arm around her. "You may be right, sweetheart. He's hurting but never says why."

Chapter 21

K at settled into a chair at the conference table and spread her material out, studying what both she and Micah had come up with.

"Do you have that list of names, Micah, that Jace gave you?"

"I do." He handed it to her, then pointed at the point. "Where do you want me to start?"

She stared at the board, oblivious to the movement of the men around her. Nathaniel and Murphy were there working on projects and upcoming schedules.

"Start about the middle of the board, and with the parents. Draw lines like you see on a family tree. Now, underneath, we need to put Bob and his siblings. That's right, just like that." She glanced down at her notes. "Now, draw a line a bit longer to Bob and connect his wife to him. To her name, connect her siblings."

She started at the board, then suddenly reached for some notes she had made. "Okay, now let's see where we go from here. Did we print the obituary for Nancy Thomas' parents?"

He searched and handed it to her. "So, it seems as if Nancy was married before. She had a different name in the obituary. Was that what Tracker was meaning?"

Nathaniel watched, then spoke up. "She mentioned a couple of names, different than what you have there."

Kat turned to study him. "I have those, but this is different from them." She blew out a breath, frustrated. "How many names does she have, and how did I know them for over five years and not see this?"

"They hide what they don't want you to see, Kat." Murphy rose from his seat and walked over to look at her material. "See, this one? It will likely track back to one of Bob's family members, but you wouldn't have seen it if you hadn't been looking for it."

Kat nodded. "You're right." She studied the paperwork spread out on the table, then the board Micah had been writing on. "This is going to take too long working this way."

"How can we make it easier then?" Murphy leaned against the table, watching her, then lifting his eyes to Micah. "What can we do to help?"

She shook her head. "You two are busy with work stuff."

Murphy laid his hand on hers, stopping her movements. "This affects us all, Kat, whether you realize it or not. You're family now, and we take care of family first."

She raised her eyes to him, startled at his words. Searching his face, she finally nodded, finally getting it that when she married Micah, her family grew to include his team mates. "Okay, then, if you two have time. What we need to do is search through this material and find any reference to one of them. I've pulled police records, public records, land records. Take your pick. Micah, did we bring my laptop?"

"Right here, sweetheart. What are you thinking?"

"I still have an older version of that software. What I destroyed with the public version. I kept a private version, not connected to that one, for my own use with the consulting I do."

"Smart lady you have there, Micah."
Nathaniel grinned at him, then looked at the
door as it opened.

Abe and the leader for the team that
was in training that week walked in. Abe
stopped, staring at them, then at the board.
"Took over the office now, have you, Kat?"

"I have, Abe. I want this over with."

He walked over to see what she had
been working on. "Micah mentioned that
Tracker came up with some names for you,
but it looks as if you've been busy too."

"Those names helped." She pointed at
the board. "This is what we have so far.
Nathaniel and Murphy volunteered to help."
She bit at her lip, not sure if it was a good idea
that they did.

"That's good. Give me a few minutes,
and then I'll help. Kat, this is Ken. His
team's in training this week." Abe turned to
look at him. "Ken, this would be good for
your team to work on as well. I'm not sure if
you've ever met Kat Evans as she was, but
she's given seminars on how to use a family
tree to catch a crook."

Ken's keen eyes studied Kat. "I was in
her second seminar, I think it was. Glad to
see you're still doing this, Kat." He turned

back to Abe. "Why don't I go find the rest of our teams and we'll dig in. My guys are always up for a challenge." He grinned. "How about a competition, my guys against yours?"

Kat started to laugh, holding her left ribs. "Now, that's the spirit. Glad to see you again, Ken."

Late that afternoon, Frankie opened the door, looking for Micah and Kat. He stared at the number of people in the room, then walked in, looking for Kat. He found her wrapped in a blanket, sitting in Abe's chair.

"What's going on, Kat?"

She grinned up at him. "A friendly competition between teams. Abe's team is competing with Ken's team to try and solve the mystery of who attacked me and wanted the program. We've actually made progress."

"You have? How?"

She nodded at the board. "That's Bob's and Betty's family trees. We have found a lot of information out there on them. Tracker was right on with the names she gave us."

"How are you doing this? I thought you destroyed your program." Frankie was clearly puzzled.

"I did, but I have a separate version I keep just for my use, not available to anyone. I don't want that to become public knowledge, so only you, Micah, Murphy and Nathaniel know that." She paused, drawing in a deep breath. She was getting tired but wasn't ready to stop yet. "Micah said you were coming out about the voice on my phone."

"He mentioned you had a voice recording."

She reached for her phone and pulled up the recorded conversation. "If you need to take my phone, I guess you'll have to."

Frankie shook his head as he listened, eyes on Kat. "You have no idea who this is?"

She shook her head. "Do you?"

Frankie nodded. "I do. We've been looking for him for months now related to something else. I'm forwarding that conversation on to my own phone. Then I'll pass it on to the lab. This may be the break we've all been looking for."

Micah had moved over to stand behind Kat. "Will this end it, do you think, Frankie?"

"I pray it does. Now, walk me through what you have. I'd like to have copies of it if I could."

"We printed off copies of what we have so far. I would suggest you take photos of the board, as we haven't entered it all into a family tree program as yet. Murphy's working on that and will get it to you."

Ian's voice rose above the noise. "Kat, can you come here? I think I've found something new."

Kat was on her feet and at his side before he had finished his sentence. "What did you find, Ian?"

He pointed at his computer monitor. "There. Another family member that we didn't have. He goes by a totally different name. He was apparently adopted as a young child, removed from Bob's family due to abuse. He's recently come into the area and connected with his family."

Frankie stood behind Ian, noting the name. "That's great, Ian. What else do we have on him?"

"Plenty." Ian turned to stare at Kat. "Did Micah say you had a voice recording of your abductor?"

She nodded. "I do. I hadn't shut off the program I was working on."

"Then, take a listen. I have a sound bite that might help."

Kat's face paled as she listened. Micah, watching his wife's face, wrapped his arms around her.

"Is that him, Kat?"

She nodded. "It is. Where's the picture Joseph pulled from that day?" She took it, and held it up near the monitor, then turned to Frankie. "There you go, Frankie. Find him and you'll find the rest." She turned and wrapped her arms around Micah.

The men had stopped working and watched as Kat had talked to Frankie. Compassion shone through as Micah gathered Kat up in his arms and walked from the room.

"How long has it been since she was abducted?" Ken's quiet question broke through the silence.

"Around three weeks." Joseph's voice held a hint of anger. "We want this guy. He broke through our security to get to her."

Frankie took the material he was offered and headed back for the office. There was a lot of footwork that needed to be one. Once back at the office, he headed for the conference room, knowing officers would be there working.

"Eddie, Kat's come up with some material. Ian found the man who abducted her."

Eddie turned and stared at Frankie. "How'd they do that when we couldn't?"

Frankie shook his head. "I have no idea. Kat had a voice recording of him, and Ian was able to trace it. Any word from downtown on our search?"

"Wilson just called. They found out where he is, and he was headed that way. I hope and pray that they find him"

Frankie agreed. Passing the information on to the detectives working, he went on a search for Caleb, not knowing if he was still in the building. He wasn't, and Frankie made a note to catch up with him the next day.

Micah stood watching as Kat slept. The day had taken a lot from her, physically as well as emotionally and mentally. His heart broke for his wife. He turned, determination in his stride, as he went searching for Abe. A long conversation, and

they had agreed on a plan. Both knew that
Frankie and Eddie would be opposed to it, but
as Micah put it, he wanted it to end yesterday.
They both felt the ones behind the abduction
of Kat thought she was dead.

Chapter 22

Frankie stared at Micah the next morning. "Are you serious? You want to do what?"

"Hold a press conference and let them know Kat is still very much alive. They think she's dead. If we go forward with this, then we can flush them out."

"Whose bright idea was this?" Frankie was shaking his head, he couldn't believe what Micah was saying.

"Mine. Abe and I talked it over, and I spoke with Kat this morning. We have an interview scheduled for this afternoon."

"Can you please put it off for a day? Wilson's downtown, and he has a suspect cornered in a building. They're going in to bring him out in about thirty minutes."

Micah shook his head. "Not happening, Frankie. It's been too long now. We need this over with and over with yesterday."

Frankie looked past Micah. "Jace, you're here. What do you have?"

"This. It's the names and addresses of all the names we've been looking at. I heard Bob Thomas passed away last night. He's never really been on the radar for this. What Tracker and I have found out is that his brother, George, found out about the program. Some cop with loose lips talked where he shouldn't have. We've passed that information on to his chief. George has been tracking Kat for years, trying to get close enough to catch her on her own. The time was right this fall."

Micah stared at him. "All because someone spoke when and where they shouldn't have? Kat was endangered and almost killed because of that?" He had to tamp down the anger he could feel building inside him.

Jace nodded. "Tracker's taken care of that officer. What you have there should be enough for your people to go through, Frankie, and come up with sufficient information for search warrants and arrest warrants." He turned to Micah. "This is the dangerous time, Micah. You need to make sure she is never alone, and I would say have two or three with her at all times. You're a target, too, remember, so you'll need to watch yourself as well."

Frankie reached for the material and scanned through it. "Are you two sure you don't want to come work for us full time? Between you and Abe's team, you've done our work for us."

Jace laughed. "Not a chance, Frankie. I love my freedom too much."

Micah watched him walk away, then turned to Frankie. "Will you have enough to end this now?"

Frankie nodded. "It looks like we will. So, will you cancel your interview for at least a couple of days, please?"

Micah stared at him, then abruptly nodded. "Two days, Frankie. That's all you get. Then, we do the interview. Kat's not going to be happy having to put it off."

"I know she's not. Listen, Micah, you two will need to be very careful over the next couple of days, at least until we get things wrapped up."

Micah turned to leave, with an "I know we will" carrying back over his shoulder.

Kat started at her husband. "What do you mean, postpone the interview?"

"Jace came in when I was talking with Frankie. He's found all the information Frankie needs to make the arrests. I told Frankie he had two days, then we would go ahead with the interview."

"I'm not happy about this, Micah. And you say he told you to have two or three people with us at all times? How do we manage that? You have to work. I can't be smothered."

Micah pulled her over close to him from where she had been perched on the couch. "I know, sweetheart. I know. Abe's trying to work something out. I still think we should have done the interview, but I felt we had to give Frankie a chance."

She nodded. "I know. I just want this over." She leaned her head back to look up at him. "How do I go to the weddings if this is still going on? Who do I put at risk?"

"We'll work something out, Kat. They all want you there. You're family to them now."

Abe looked up as Murphy and Matt approached him.

"You two look very serious. What's up?"

The two men exchanged a glance, then Murphy spoke.

"We just talked to Micah. Jace has provided all kinds of information to Frankie that should end in all, if not most, of the arrests. Micah and Kat aren't happy with having to wait, though."

"And Frankie's afraid they'll do something, or else someone will find them." Abe spoke their thoughts aloud. "What do we do, guys? We can't be there all the time."

Matt nodded. "He still wants to do the interview but agreed to give Frankie two days. I just hope that's sufficient time."

"And Kat's worried about coming to the weddings, putting us and our families at risk."

Abe stared at the wall in front of him, not seeing it. "I agree with her, that she will put us at risk. We'll manage somehow."

Abe looked towards the door as it opened. "Frankie, what are you doing out here?"

Frankie looked harried. "We've arrested almost all of the ones we were looking for. Bob's brother is still at large. We've been told he's headed this way. I have patrol officers around your site as much as I can, but there's still room for him to get through to you. It's been done before."

Abe was on his feet, heading for the door, Murphy and Matt on his heels. "Matt, you head for Micah's. Get them into the safe room, now."

Micah looked at Matt as he explained what was happening, a stunned look on his face. "He's here somewhere?"

Matt nodded. "Abe wants you two in the safe room now."

Micah turned. "Kat's sleeping. I'll need to wake her."

"I don't think you'll have time, Micah." Matt had barely finished his words when he was shoved forward, just missing Micah.

The men spun to stare at the man standing inside the door, slamming and locking it behind him. A weapon in his hand, he pointed towards the living room.

"In there. Where's the woman?"

"Who are you?"

"Doesn't matter. Bring the woman out here."

Micah shook his head. "That's not happening." He heard the faint sound of a window from the back of the house and exchanged a quick glance with Matt, who nodded. Micah was hoping that Kat had managed to get out.

Kat picked herself up from the ground she had dropped to, tears in her eyes at the pain she felt. She prayed for Micah, and she was sure Matt, who were locked in the house with that madman. She turned and covered her mouth to keep from screaming out loud as she almost ran into Doug. Doug's finger was at his mouth, and then he pointed towards Abe's house. Nathaniel was there, grasping her hand and moving her towards the hidden opening to the safe room.

Doug pointed at the open window, and two of his men slipped through, taking up positions where they could hear what was going on in the house. Doug and the rest of his men spread out around the house, ready to enter when they were given the word.

Abe and the rest of his team stood back, geared up and ready to help. He knew Nathaniel had Kat safe. Now to make sure Micah and Matt were safe.

Micah stared at the man standing in front of him, eyes narrowed as he watched. He knew Matt was doing the same, assessing for an opportunity to take him down. He prayed that Kat had made it safely to Abe's and into the safe room.

The man paced, weapon wavering in his hand. He muttered to himself, every few seconds staring at the men. He finally stopped.

"Where is she? Get her out here."

"She's not here." Micah's voice rang with confidence. He prayed that God would be there, would take over and keep them safe.

"Oh, yes, she is. I've been watching. She hasn't left this house."

Micah shrugged, moving slightly away from Matt. "Well, you're wrong. Go ahead. Search the house. You won't find her."

"You're lying." He pointed his weapon once more at Micah. "Get her out here."

Micah shook his head. "No. She's not in the house." He dropped to the floor as did Matt as he saw the man's finger tighten on his weapon.

The weapon discharged. As the sound of it faded, the two ETF members appeared, shouting for the man to put down his weapon. He stared at them in shock, then turned his weapon towards them. They had no choice. Gunfire echoed, and the man was down.

Micah and Matt slowly picked themselves up from the floor and were hurried from the house. It was now a crime scene and they needed to be away from it. Abe appeared next to them, pointing to his house.

Micah stopped outside Abe's house and stared back at his own, somewhat in shock at what had gone down. He was just so thankful neither he or Matt had been hurt. Ian approached.

"In the house, Micah. We don't know if there are any more of his comrades around."

Micah nodded and headed inside, eyes scanning the area. Ian stopped at the door and searched the rocky area around them. It had held danger for them before.

Kat paced the safe room, worried for Micah. The voice had awakened her from her nap, and she had slipped out the window, knowing Micah would want that. She had hated to leave him but had felt a sense of relief when she saw Doug and his team, and then Nathaniel.

"How long, Nathaniel?"

He shrugged from where he was standing, shoulder against the wall. "We don't know. Someone will come get us when it's safe."

"Have you used this room before? It's set up to be comfortable."

Nathaniel nodded. "We have. Adriel was one of the ladies we had down here." He paused as he heard a noise at the basement entrance, and then the door opened.

Ian stood in the entry and nodded at the question in Nathaniel's eyes. Nathaniel relaxed, knowing Micah and Matt were safe.

"Want to go find your guy, Kat?" Ian smiled at her. "He's upstairs."

"He's safe? Matt, too?" At his nod, she brushed by him and ran for the stairs. Searching among the men in the house, she saw Micah and ran for him and wrapped her arms around him, sobs of relief coming.

Micah surrounded her with his arms, and his head went down on her, his tears wetting her hair.

After a few minutes, Kat leaned back. "Is it over finally, Micah?"

He looked up at Caleb, who nodded. "It is, Kat. It is. Caleb's people will be working through everything over the next few weeks. But you're safe now."

He felt the relief that flowed through her body and caught her up into his arms when she collapsed. Matt was there, pointing to one of the bedrooms on the main floor.

Sarah searched the men in Abe's home. Luke had come for her, telling that Matt was alright and in Abe's home. Matt turned as he felt a body hit his.

"Matt!" Sarah's voice was muffled against him.

"I'm okay, sweetheart. Everyone's okay. It's all over now for Micah and Kat."

She leaned back to look up at him. "It's all over?" At his nod, she spoke. "Thank God it is. And thank Him that he protected you two and Kat tonight.

Chapter 23

Caleb looked around the conference room ten days later. The investigation was winding down and would soon be in the hands of the prosecutors. It was a mess, he thought, a real mess. He was thankful that Kat had survived her ordeal. It had been so close for her.

He turned as Eddie approached. "Ready to head out for Abe's?"

Caleb nodded. "I am. This has been a nasty bit of business."

"It has," Eddie agreed as they turned to walk through the department building.

Kat paced, waiting for the two officers to arrive. Her thoughts went to Bob and wondered how he had been involved, if he had been at all. She also wondered if they would ever know that.

Micah watched from the doorway he was standing in. He turned as Abe touched his shoulder, then moved past him to his office. His team mates and their ladies were gathering to hear what Caleb and Eddie had to share with them. He knew there was somethings they couldn't, but they would and could share what they had.

Eddie searched the faces of the men and women gathered in Abe's home. They were all affected by this time of trouble. He waited for Caleb to speak.

Caleb took watched the men and their ladies, then turned his eyes to Abe, the only one without a lady. He watched for a minute, then turned as a knock came to the door, and Jace entered. He nodded. Everyone was here that should be, except for Tracker, and she had absolutely refused to come.

"It's been quite an adventure you've had, Kat." Caleb's keen eyes watched as her face whitened and she nodded. "As far as we can determine, Bob was never involved. Where it all started was back when an officer at one of your early seminars said something he shouldn't have, and word got out on the street. Bob's brother got involved. He's the one who was sending you the text messages all along. Bob's wife is the one who sent you the packages recently. She was trying to scare you into leaving, thinking if you did, then Bob's brother would leave, and they would be safe. Unfortunately, she's been involved in criminal activities over the years, and now she'll be facing those charges. Your abductor was the one who was killed. Bob's brother was the one who tried to get you to bring up the program. He had agreed to get it for a criminal family. He was the one who was outside your hospital room. His sister is the woman you heard outside the room you were held in. She's been arrested.

"It all came down to money, Kat. I'm sorry you had to go through what you did. Greed and depravity drove them."

Kat nodded. "That's what Micah and I felt all along. I'm just glad it's over, and now we can go on with our lives." She looked up at Micah sitting beside her. "I just want to say I'm sorry each one of you had to go through what you did protecting me. Jace, thank you to Tracker and yourself for what you did."

Jace smiled. "I just wish you hadn't had to destroy your program, Kat."

"It wasn't worth anyone else's life, Jace. God used it when it was up. When it was time for it to go, I had His peace knowing that the truth would come through somehow."

She looked up at Caleb and Eddie. "Caleb, please thank your team for me. They certainly went above and beyond in their search."

Caleb smiled. "I will do that very thing, Kat."

The couples separated, the women staying in the living room, talk turning to the upcoming weddings.

The men headed for the business office. Abe wanted to debrief his men. All seven had been through life-threatening situations in the past few months, and he wanted to ensure they were dealing with it. They all assured him that they were. Talk then turned to work and what was upcoming.

As the men stood to leave, Murphy stayed back, watching Abe.

"Abe, are you really okay?" The two men had been friends since their first day of college.

Abe shrugged. "I guess I am. I'm glad you and your ladies are safe."

"That's not what I meant, Abe. You've had something buried for years. I remember your Dad and Eddie going away and then coming back with you. As physically hurt as you were, you've just buried everything inside. You need to talk to someone."

Abe studied his friend, then sighed. "I know, Murphy. I know. It's just so complicated though and involves someone else."

Murphy nodded. "I get that, Abe. Just know I'm praying for you."

Kat found Micah later that day, standing in the doorway of the home they had shared. Work was underway to repair and replace what had been damaged. She wrapped her arms around him.

"God was good, Micah."

He turned and kissed her. "He was, sweetheart. When I thought I was losing you, I didn't know how I would go on."

"We go on in His strength and His power and His truth." She turned. "Come, I have dinner ready for us."

Three months later, Micah was on a mission, a mission to find his missing wife. She wasn't in their home. His eyes searched the area around them, then headed for the lake. She had a favourite rock there she liked to sit on and think about life.

Kat looked up as Micah sat beside her.

"You've been quiet the last few days, Kat." Micah stared across the lake. "What's up? That's not like you."

Kat wrapped her arms around his and leaned on him. "Just a lot to think about. I'm decided not to give any more seminars or do any teaching. My consultation work is almost more than I can handle at times."

"You just need to decide who you want to help and set up boundaries for yourself. But that's not all, is it?" His eyes watched the face of the woman he loved.

"No, it's not. I'm been thinking a lot the last few days of what we went through.

God was good, Micah. He allowed the truth to come out. With the trials over, I'm glad to know that my faith in Bob wasn't in vain."

Micah nodded. "That's true."

Kat was silent for a moment. "You know, one thing we've never really discussed is having children."

Micah stopped his movements and waited for her to continue. When she didn't, he spoke. "No, we haven't. Is there something you want to tell me?"

She smiled. "I guess I have to. We'll be parents in a few months, Micah, and that scares me."

Micah wrapped his arms around his wife, tears in his eyes. "I'm so glad I have you. Just know that any child of ours will be raised to love and trust in God."

She turned her face up to him. "That I know, Micah. You are the head of this house, as is Biblical, in your leadership in our faith. Thank you."

He dropped a kiss on her, then hugged her tight. "You're the helpmeet God prepared for me."

They stood and walked hand in hand back to their home. They had some planning to do, but first their hearts were raised to their heavenly Father in thanks.

Dear Readers:

Thank you for choosing to read the story of Micah and Kat. Greed and depravity came through in the men who were after her computer program. Does such a program exist or could it? I have no idea. This was just something I chose to use in the story.

I have had an interest in my family tree for years, which I shared with my Mom, tracing her family back to Ireland and my Dad's to England. If you wonder at the Irish that comes through in my stories, my DNA through Ancestry.com showed I am 65% Irish.

God's truth is something that I think we can struggle with at times. We don't always want to hear what He has to say, but we need to listen and learn and follow.

God bless each one of you on your journey with Him.

Ronna

PRAISE FOR V. ROMAS BURTON

I knew Heartmender was a winner when, after reading mountains of other books, this was the one I kept thinking about.

— S. C. MEGALE, NEXT GENERATION INDIE
BOOK AWARDS

V. Romas Burton's *Heartmender* pumps new blood into the classic good-versus-evil paradigm by way of the classic Seven Deadly Sins.

— LOREHAVEN MAGAZINE

This is a perfect combination of fairy-tale and Christian fantasy that I absolutely adore.

— M. H., AMAZON

Though Addie's story is only fictional, her journey testifies to us that there are forces of light and darkness around us. That we can choose to be "mended" by someone greater than us and who loves and cares for us.

— LAURA, BARNES & NOBLE

This is one of the best allegories I've ever read.

— ANGELA, INSTAGRAM

We feel, taste, smell all the different challenges faced with great description.

— JASON, AMAZON

It was frightening and beautiful, a tale of the war between good and evil and our parts in the fight.

— DAWN, AMAZON

Highly recommended for those who love light romance, action/adventure, sibling stories, christian allegory that's done in a very relatable, not overbearing/heavy handed way.

— CLAIRE, AMAZON

Narnia meets Dante's Inferno.

— KELL, GOODREADS

Addie is a flawed yet dynamic character I couldn't help but root for.

— ANGIE, GOODREADS

A deliciously dark world sprinkled with Hope.

— RACHAEL, GOODREADS

I read it breathlessly racing along as fast as the main character did.

— MAURA, GOODREADS

I devoured the new world created by the author.

— SOFIA, GOODREADS

The artistry is hauntingly surreal yet truthful for its depiction of a young woman who must overcome the trials of life that blindside so many of us.

— LANDS UNCHARTED

This has been one of the greatest books I've had the pleasure of reading this year.

— JEFF, GOODREADS

A very unique take on the seven deadly sins, and the choices we all face throughout our lives.

— CHRISSY, AMAZON

Decim
Patet
Ocean
R
Wintertide
Shalley Mou
The Market
Barracks